HICCUP HADDOCK HORRENDOUS THE THIRD JUST WANTS A NICE PEACEFUL BIRTHDAY.

But Hiccup's dad wants to steal the prized HOW TO TRAIN YOUR DRAGON book, and prove that his Hooligans are just as good as the Bog Burglars – except Hiccup's dragon Toothless has **EATEN** it!

So when Camicazi suggests stealing a copy from the grim Meathead Public Library, it seems like a good idea. **BUT IT ISN'T!**

The library is guarded by the Horrible Hairy Scary Librarian, four hundred Meathead Warrior Guards **AND** their Driller-Dragons . . .

Will Hiccup survive – or is he **DOOMED** on his own birthday?

ALSO INCLUDES A DRAGONESE DICTIONARY

You don't **HAVE** to read the Hiccup books in order.
But if you want to, this is the right order:

1. How to train your Dragon
2. How to be a Pirate
3. How to speak Dragonese
4. How to Cheat a Dragon's Curse
5. How to Twist a Dragon's Tale
6. A Hero's Guide to Deadly Dragons
7. How to Ride a Dragon's Storm
8. How to Break a Dragon's Heart
9. How to Steal a Dragon's Sword
10. How to Seize a Dragon's Jewel
11. How to Betray a Dragon's Hero
12. How to Fight a Dragon's Fury

A Hero's Guide to Deadly Dragons

written and illustrated by

CRESSIDA COWELL

Hodder
Children's
Books

A division of Hachette Children's Group

CONTENTS

How NOT to Celebrate Your Birthday

THE ISLE OF BERK
Hooligan ship
Caliban Caves
(Do NOT go here unless you have to)
Unlandable Cove
DEATH'S HEAD HEADLAND
Wild Dragon Cliff
Hooligan Village
Madman's Gully
THE HIGHEST POINT (recently destroyed by FIRE)
Hooligan Harbour
The Long Beach
Black Heart Bay
The Little Isles
Cowrie Beach
Puffin Point
Hysterical ship
Isles of DOOM
Wanderer ship
outcast ship
Bashem-Oik ship
Bog-Burglar ship
Visithug ship

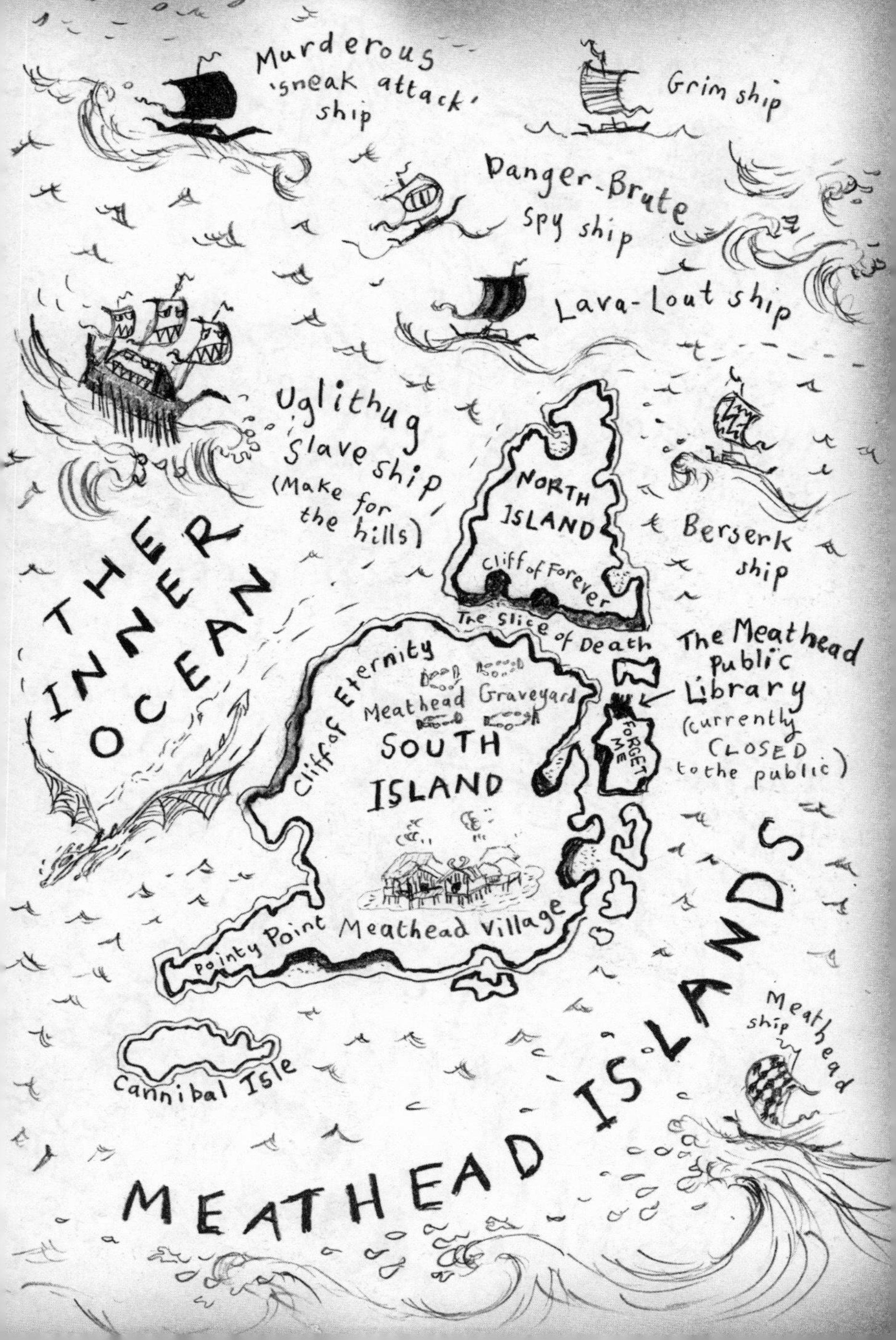

Murderous 'sneak attack' ship

Grim ship

Danger-Brute spy ship

Lava-Lout ship

Uglithug Slave ship (Make for the hills)

NORTH ISLAND

Cliff of Forever

Berserk ship

THE INNER OCEAN

The Slice of Death

The Meathead Public Library (currently (CLOSED to the public)

FORGET ME

Cliff of Eternity

Meathead Graveyard

SOUTH ISLAND

Pointy Point   Meathead Village

Cannibal Isle

Meathead ship

MEATHEAD ISLANDS

THE OPEN OCEAN

(Home of the Mighty Monsters,
Seadragonus Giganticus
the Doomfang, the Darkbreather)

sky burial place
MOUNT MURDEROUS

THE MURDEROUS MOUNTAINS

Hero's End

WRECKER'S BAY

Reef Warrior Terr

THE REEF

To America
(if there
is such
a place)

The Summer Current

TOMORROW

NOTHIN
THE FROZEN ISLE OF NOWHERE
OVING ISLANDS OF ICE
ICE GORGES
The Winter Wind
VISITHUGY TERRITORY
GRIMBEARD'S DESPAIR
THE BARBARIC ARCHIPELAGO
BASHEM
Isle of the Skullions
PUFFIN ISLES
The Sullen Sea
SILENCE
VILLAINY
Bog-Burglar Islands
THE WRATH OF THOR
HYSTERIA
LAVA-LOUT ISLAND
THE DUNGEONS OF THE DANGER-BRUTES
SWALLOW
Beware Slitherfangs
THE SWALLOWING SANDS

NOTHING
PREVARICATION POINT
THE DRAGON'S NOSE
THE OUTCAST LANDS
THE BARBARIC ARCHIPELAGO
THE BAY OF THE BROKEN HEART
Isle of BERK
THE PEACEABLE COUNTRY
THE ISLAND of the QUIET LIFE
The Sea-Known-as Woden's-Bathtub
Meathead Islands
The Summer Current
THE MAZY MULTITUDES
BERSERK
THE WOODS THAT HOWLE
THE MYSTERY
THE WATERLANDS
ROMAN EMPIRE this way

THE HAUNTED MARSHES

THE GORGE OF THE THUNDER BOLT OF THOR

THE MAINLAND

THE FLASHBURN SCHOOL OF SWORDFIGHTING

THE DRAGON HATCHING GROUNDS OF 'BLOODSPILT' BAY

THE FLAMING FOREST

THE UGLI-THUG STAVELANDS
(Abandon hope, all ye who enter here)

This is

HICCUP HORRENDOUS Haddock the Third, the HOPE and THE HEIR to the HAIRY Hooligan Tribe....

Hiccup is a Viking, and is on his first year of the Pirate Training Programme, which is a bit like prison but the boys are armed and the food is TRULY DISGUSTING.

Vikings are the Terrors of the Seas, the Scourge of Civilisation, great Barbarian Warriors of the North.

But what Hiccup is is mostly WET.

It rains a lot on the Isle of Berk.

Did you know, there are 101 different words for 'rain' in the **Dragonese** language?

Hiccup knows them ALL.

dragon wings make an excellent umbrella

This is Hiccup's dragon,

TOOTHLESS

He is the smallest hunting dragon anybody has ever seen. And he hasn't got any teeth. But he can still give a nasty bite with his VERY HARD gums, as you will find out if you ever try and take back the haddock he's just sneakily stolen from your plate when you weren't looking.

NEVER try and take back the haddock. You might need all *ten* of your fingers one day, for swordfighting, or learning to play the harp or something.

Sometimes Hiccup can't help wishing Toothless was a truly gigantic Monstrous Nightmare kind of dragon… but don't tell him.

This is Hiccup's father,

THE CHIEF of the HAIRY HOoLigan TRiBE, Stoick THE VAST, oh HEAR HiS NAME and TREMBLE UGH UGH

As you can see, he is tough but not all that bright.

VALHaLLaRama

Hiccup's mother is a great Hero
who is often away questing.
This is Hiccup as a baby
looking at her armour.

This is Hiccup's best friend

FiSHLegS

His dragon, Horrorcow, is
a normal size, but she is
vegetarian and not very scary
unless you happen to be a
carrot.

Things Fishlegs often
says in a life-threatening
situation:

'For Thor's sake, I can't believe we are out here
surrounded by deadly fire-breathing carnivores YET
AGAIN, call me fussy but I quite fancied staying alive
until I was at least twelve...'

CaMicaZi

is the daughter of
Big-Boobied Bertha,
the Chief of the
Bog-Burglars.
Hiccup never tells her
this, because Camicazi
is way too pleased with

herself already, but she IS a very good swordfighter.

She is also handy at Burglary, and here she is in her Burglary Suit. Some of that equipment looks illegal.

Things Camicazi often says when swordfighting a large and scary Cannibal:

'Ooooh you're just TERRIBLE at this, really TERRIBLE… I hope you're better at eating people than you are at swordfighting, because if you're not you must be STARVING… LOOK!' (cuts a large letter C in the shirtfront of the Cannibal with the tip of her sword) 'C is for Camicazi, *and* Clumsy, Cowardly, Cockroach of a Cannibal, I could have killed you five times already, it's PATHETIC.'

You can recognise **Snotlout** from a mile off by his enormous hairy nostrils, they are GIGANTIC, you could park a Gronckle up there.

And here are some others…

clueless

THE Hairy Scary Librarian

DOGSBREATH THE DUHBRAIN

FIREWORM
Snotlout's dragon

GOBBER
THE
BELCH → teacher in charge
of the Pirate
Training Programme

Madguts the Murderous (not a nice man)

Gumboil Madguts's lovely assistant

BIG-BOOBIED BERTHA (chief of the Bog-Burglars)

Stormfly

sniff sniff

HOW *NOT* TO CELEBRATE YOUR BIRTHDAY

Hiccup and his
sword, Endeavour

Once there were dragons.

Imagine a time of DRAGONS – some larger than mountainsides, slumbering in the depths of the ocean; some smaller than your fingernail, hopping through the heather.

Imagine a time of VIKING HEROES, in which men were men and women were sort of men too and even some little babies had chest hair.

And now imagine that you are a boy called Hiccup Horrendous Haddock the Third, not yet twelve years old and not yet turning out to be the kind of Hero his father would have liked him to be. That boy of course, was really ME, but the boy I was then seems so far away to me now that I shall tell this story almost as if he were a stranger.

So, imagine that instead of being me, this stranger, this Hero-in-Waiting, is YOU.

You are small. You have red hair. You don't realise it yet, but you are about to set out on the most alarming episode of your life so far... When you are an old, old man like I am you will call it *How NOT to Celebrate Your Birthday* – and even at this distance in time it will still cause your old wrinkled arms to prickle with goose bumps as you remember the perils and dangers of that terrifying adventure...

1. AN ODD WAY TO SPEND YOUR BIRTHDAY

At exactly twelve o'clock a.m. on the morning of his twelfth birthday, Hiccup Horrendous Haddock the Third, the Hope and Heir to the Tribe of the Hairy Hooligans, was standing shakily on a windy, narrow window ledge three hundred feet up in the air.

Hiccup was a rather ordinary looking boy for someone with such a long and impressive name; a small-ish, thin-ish, runner-bean of a boy with bright red hair that shot straight up as if it was surprised, and a face that nobody ever remembered.

His knees were wobbling as he flattened himself against the wall.

The window ledge that he was perching on belonged to a Castle of terrifying size and spookiness which sprawled like an ugly black monster on top of the gull-shrieking cliffs of the little Isle of Forget Me.

Although this Castle was known as THE MEATHEAD PUBLIC LIBRARY, it was not, in fact, open to the general public. This was back in Viking times, when books were considered a highly dangerous civilising influence, so they were rounded up and kept

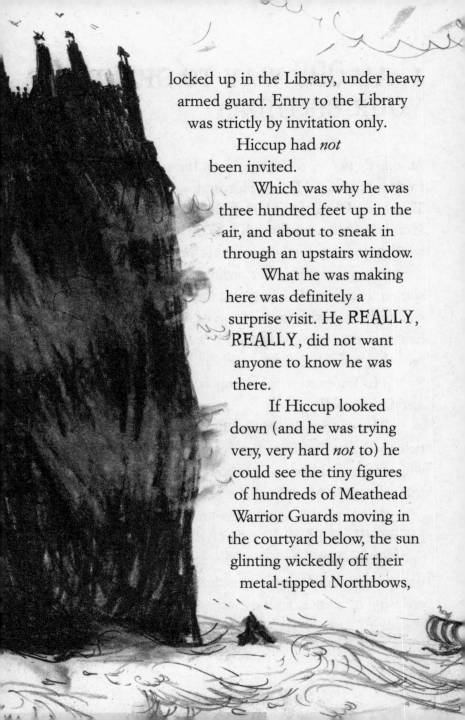

locked up in the Library, under heavy
armed guard. Entry to the Library
was strictly by invitation only.

Hiccup had *not*
been invited.

Which was why he was
three hundred feet up in the
air, and about to sneak in
through an upstairs window.

What he was making
here was definitely a
surprise visit. He REALLY,
REALLY, did not want
anyone to know he was
there.

If Hiccup looked
down (and he was trying
very, very hard *not* to) he
could see the tiny figures
of hundreds of Meathead
Warrior Guards moving in
the courtyard below, the sun
glinting wickedly off their
metal-tipped Northbows,

their Driller-Dragons on long chains beside them. Hiccup knew that they only had to look up, and they would have no hesitation at all in shooting on sight.

Hiccup swallowed hard. He was nerving himself up to climb through the broken window and into the Library – but he didn't really want to do this, either.

Who knew **WHAT** could be hidden in that dark maze of rooms, a labyrinth so huge that you could be lost in there for weeks without a soul ever finding you?

Whatever *else* was in there, Hiccup knew that somewhere in that terrifying book-warren there prowled the Hairy Scary Librarian himself, the half-blind, half-dumb Guardian of the Library.

Master Swordsman, Mathematical Genius and an all-round scary individual, the Hairy Scary Librarian showed no mercy to Intruders.

Hiccup had heard him at gatherings of the Tribes, boasting of how he finished off foolish Warriors who dared to try and find out the Library's secret with one slash of his swords, which he called his 'Heart-Slicers'.

'I croaks them with me Heart-Slicers,' he would whisper, with the

firelight flickering on his undead eyes. 'I unzips them from their goggle-screams to their grub-washers.'
Then he would make a nasty swiping motion from his throat down to his belly button. 'Serves them right – NOBODY borrows books from MY Library and lives to tell the tale.'

And if the Hairy Scary Librarian was scary even on a social occasion, when you were sitting down at a cosy campfire with the rest of the Tribe all comfortably settled around you, how much scarier still was he when he was doing his business, lurking like a spider round every corner of his spooky Library, his Heart-Slicers at the ready?

Particularly when, like Hiccup, you had come to the Library not just to stroll about, but to actually STEAL one of the precious books and take it home with you.

At that moment, a small wild dragon happened to fly past the spot where Hiccup was perching. Hiccup followed it automatically with his eyes. 'Lesser-Spotted Squirrelserpent,' Hiccup said to himself. And as the little dragon soared, free and careless, with nothing to do and nowhere to go, into the bright blue sky, Hiccup thought to himself: *What AM I doing? This is my BIRTHDAY, for Thor's sake. I should be*

sitting at home enjoying myself instead of risking my neck three hundred feet up a Library of Doom...What AM I DOING? HOW DID I GET MYSELF INTO THIS MESS IN THE FIRST PLACE? *NOTHING could possibly be worse than this.*

And at that moment, Hiccup was so busy with this thought and with watching the Lesser-Spotted Squirrelserpent wheeling through the air in a lazy arc, that he lost concentration, and his foot slipped on the crumbly edge of the window. And with a smothered shriek, he fell off the ledge.

He fell off the ledge entirely, arms and legs scrabbling wildly, and one flailing hand just caught on to the window ledge as he fell... and held – leaving him hanging by one hand, with nothing between him and the hard ground but three hundred feet of pure clear air. Hiccup screamed again.

Down below on the battlements, the heads of four hundred Meathead Guards tipped upwards to look. All four hundred reached for their Northbows.

And, floating up to Hiccup as he swung from the ledge with one hand, came the ominous sound of the Driller-Dragons setting their drills a-whirring.

2. SPINACH WITH YOUR DRIFTWOOD?

We'll just leave Hiccup hanging off the window-frame, shall we, while we go back and discover exactly how he got himself into this mess in the first place.

When Hiccup had woken up at seven o'clock that morning, he had absolutely no idea of what he would be doing only five hours after.

He was rather excited, because it was his birthday, and although he was twelve years old, in fact technically speaking it was only his THIRD birthday, for Hiccup had been born on the 29th of February, a Leap Year.

His first thought, when he woke up, was to make a wish. And this wish was, 'Please, Thor, could you make this a nice, quiet, PEACEFUL day? No shipwrecks, no storms, no close encounters with homicidal villains with hooks for hands, or with the deadlier type of dragon? Just for my birthday?'

From this you may gather that peaceful days in the Archipelago were few and far between, and the life of a would-be Viking Hero was exciting, if exhausting.

Hiccup got up, and spent some time persuading

his pet dragon, Toothless, to eat a healthy breakfast.

Dragons are supposed to eat plenty of vegetables, and, weirdly, lots of WOOD, small branches, twigs, the bark of trees. This seems to help their fire-breathing, and this is very important because a dragon who can't breathe fire gets very sick indeed, and eventually explodes.

Toothless was a rather disobedient Common-or-Garden dragon, unusual only in that he was a lot smaller than all the other boys' dragons. He hadn't eaten his wood for weeks, and now he absolutely refused to eat either his spinach or his driftwood, and just sat in front of his plate blowing grumpy smoke rings.

'OK, then, Toothless,' said Hiccup, 'if you're going to be like this, I'm just going to go to the Burglary Competition without you. But when I come back, you better have eaten up ALL that driftwood or else there will be NO HADDOCK.'

'You is a very m-m-mean Master,'

35

said Toothless with dignity, 'and your heart is made out of bogeys.'*

In a big sulk, he climbed back into the bowl of spinach and sank down into it, like a very small crocodile into a mudbank. Only his nose and tail were showing, so it looked like the bowl of spinach was blowing smoke rings. Toothless swished his tail and spinach sprayed everywhere.

Hiccup went off to the Pick-Pocketing Finals of the Burglary Competition.

A nearby Tribe called the Bog-Burglars was visiting the Hooligans, and the Burglary Competition had been carrying on for the previous three days. The Bog-Burglars were frighteningly good in the Burglary Department, as their name suggests. They had already won the Sheep-Rustling Competition on the first day, and the Narrowboat-Nicking Competition on the second day.

This was the final day of the Competition, the Pick-Pocketing Challenge, and the Hooligans needed to win this to salvage some pride.

Unfortunately the Bog-Burglars were just as good

---

*Hiccup and Toothless were speaking in Dragonese, the language that dragons speak to each other. There have been very, very few humans over the centuries who have been able to speak this interesting language, and Hiccup was one of them.

at pick-pocketing as they were at everything else, and yet again the Hooligans were thoroughly beaten in the match.

Hiccup had a particularly gloomy time in the Competition. Not only did he completely FAIL in the Burglary department, but his unpleasant cousin, Snotlout, had made some very sneering remarks about his birthday in front of everybody else: 'So the ickle baby Hiccup is three years old today, is he?' he had jeered. 'Trust a WEIRDO like you, Hiccup, to be born on the WEIRDEST day of the year... and bad luck for us that a FAILURE like you was ever born at all. If it wasn't for you, I would be the next Chief of the Hooligan Tribe, and a very brilliant and violent Chief I would be too... Burgle his shirt, Dogsbreath!'

And Snotlout's sidekick Dogsbreath the Duhbrain, a brute of a boy with a ring through his nose and very limited communication skills, had removed Hiccup's shirt, and smooshed him into the mud.

'Everybody else may be *celebrating* your birthday at this Birthday Banquet this evening,' Snotlout had snarled, 'but *I* am wearing BLACK, because I am *mourning* the fact that you were ever born at all... Have a Miserable Third Birthday, Hiccup THE USELESS!'

It was all very depressing.

A disappointed, dishevelled, and mud-splattered Hiccup got back again three hours later, with his friends Fishlegs and Camicazi.

Fishlegs was a Hooligan like Hiccup, but he looked more like a daddy-long-legs with asthma and a squint. Camicazi was a very small, blonde Bog-Burglar, and she had hair as untouched by human hand as parts of the Amazonian rainforest.

Despite her size, Camicazi was PARTICULARLY good at pick-pocketing, and she was carrying five Hooligan daggers, three Hooligan helmets of various different sizes, and a pair of Stoick the Vast's hairy underpants.

'I can't THINK how you got them off him without him noticing,' Hiccup was saying, with reluctant admiration. Stoick the Vast was Hiccup's father, a classic Viking of the traditional 'large and terrifying' type. 'He's going to hit the roof when he finds out…'

'Oh it was easy peasy lemon-squeezy,' boasted Camicazi, carelessly twiddling one of the daggers. (If Camicazi had a fault, it was that she *did* have a tendency to be rather pleased with herself.) 'He can't see a thing through that beard of his. I could have taken the shirt and the trousers off him as well if I'd wanted to.'

'Well, thank Thor you didn't,' said Hiccup with
huge relief. 'It would have put him in an even worse bate
than he is already. I'm going to have to tiptoe round him
for the next couple of days, as it is, so as not to get into
trouble.'

When the three of them walked into the room,
Hiccup gasped in horror.

The room was covered in spinach.

The driftwood was sitting on the plate, untouched…

And Toothless was sitting in the middle of the room, looking rather guilty.

He had eaten three-quarters of Chief Stoick the Vast's new throne, the big one with all the carved knobbly pictures of Woden on it.

3. STOICK FAILS TO SEE THE FUNNY SIDE

At this bad moment, Stoick the Vast stomped into the room.

Hiccup's father, Stoick the Vast, O Hear His Name and Tremble, Ugh, Ugh, was the Chief of the Tribe of the Hairy Hooligans. He had a belly like a battleship, a beard like a hedgehog struck by lightning, a good heart but a short temper, and he was already in a very bad mood.

Camicazi's mother, Big-Boobied Bertha, the Chief of the Bog-Burglars, had said some very harsh, jeering words about the Hooligan performance in the Burglary Competition.

'YOU HOOLIGANS COULDN'T BURGLE YOUR WAY OUT OF A PAPER BAG!' Big-Boobied Bertha had bellowed in between laughing herself silly, and those unkind words had stung Stoick, who couldn't resist a challenge, particularly one set by Big-Boobied Bertha herself. Stoick bet her two of his finest axes that he could prove BY THE END OF THE DAY that Hooligans were *just* as good at Burglary as Bog-Burglars. Bertha had accepted, they had bumped bellies on the bet. And that was that. And it had a lot to do with why Hiccup was hanging so precariously in the Library as you will see.

Stoick was now wondering if this had been wise. Bog-Burglars, you see, were so very good at Burglary.

All in all, Stoick wasn't in the best of moods to find his brand-new throne had been burnt to a crisp.

'AAAAAAAAAAAAARGH!' screamed Stoick the Vast, tearing his beard out. 'MY FAVOURITE THRONE *DESTROYED!*'

'It's not *destroyed*, Sir,' said Fishlegs quickly, thinking on his feet. 'It's just a little black around the edges... it adds a sort of lived-in, uncivilised feel to it, you know, and that's all the rage in Viking furniture right now.'

Stoick calmed down slightly.

'Look!' said Fishlegs, shaking the chair enthusiastically, 'it still works as a CHAIR, it's just got a new feel to it.'

Stoick rubbed his beard thoughtfully.

Fishlegs patted the seat of the chair.

'Come on!' encouraged Fishlegs. 'Let's see how you look on it.'

Stoick the Vast lowered his great bottom into the chair and Fishlegs stood back.

'Bravo!' clapped Fishlegs. 'So *barbaric*! You are the very MODEL of a modern Viking General...'

'You think so?' asked Stoick, flexing his muscles.

He *did* look rather good actually, a great six-and-a-half-foot Viking Chieftain with a beard like an erupting bird's nest in this huge, burnt-out ruin of a throne, all twisted and blackened and still smoking slightly.

'Oh *yes*!' gushed Fishlegs. 'You're a vision from Valhalla! His Scariness Stoick the Vast, Most High Chieftain of the Hairy Hooligan Tribe, O Hear His Name and Tremble, Ugh, Ugh, at his most frightening... Primitive! Magnificent! Terri—'

The left back leg of the throne shivered and collapsed.

His Scariness Stoick the Vast, Most High Chieftain of the Hairy Hooligan Tribe, O Hear His Name and Tremble, Ugh, Ugh, fell to the floor with a crash that shook the house to its rafters.

There was a nasty pause.

Fishlegs opened his mouth – I'm not sure how even *Fishlegs* was going to talk them out of this one. But Camicazi spoilt it anyway.

Most people would be far too scared to laugh at the Chief of the Hairy Hooligans, but unfortunately

Bog-Burglars aren't afraid of anything. Camicazi LAUGHED SO HARD she nearly fell over.

Stoick leapt to his feet with a quickness surprising in someone who was built like a bull on a body-building programme.

Stoick lost his temper.

And when a Hooligan loses his temper, he *really* loses it.

'**SILENCE!**' roared Stoick. 'HOW *DARE* YOU LAUGH AT **ME**, YOU MINUSCULE LITTLE FEMALE MARSH-MEDDLER?'

It was at this moment that he realised that the minuscule little female marsh-meddler was holding a rather smart pair of hairy underpants that looked strangely familiar... Thunderbolts of Thor! She'd had the sheer Bog-Burglar cheek to snaffle his smalls!

Swelling up like an infuriated baboon, he snatched the furry pants. 'AND HOW *DARE* YOU NICK THE KNICKERS OF THE CHIEF OF THE HAIRY HOOLIGAN TRIBE!' roared Stoick the Vast.

'It was a pick-pocketing competition,' grinned Camicazi cheekily. 'In case you Hooligans hadn't noticed...'

Although perfectly true, this wasn't a remark that was likely to put Stoick in a better frame of mind.

ADVANCED BURGLARY TIPS from CAMICAZI

Burgling from Grabbit the Grim.

A steady hand is essential for all Burglary Exercises. Quick wits are as important as nimble fingers, as demonstrated HERE →

fig 1.

Gently remove his helmet, approaching from above.

fig 2.

Softly remove swords and sandals, approaching from below

If you get caught SHEEP-RUSTLING: ACT SURPRISED.

'Oh, my goodness! You're right, there IS a sheep on my head! Well, I have **ABSOLUTELY NO IDEA** how *that* could have got there...'

fig 3. Your victim realises he has been BURGLED.

A quick getaway is ALWAYS a good idea...

'A CHIEF'S UNDERWEAR IS SACRED
ROYAL PROPERTY!' howled Stoick the Vast. 'AS
IS HIS THRONE! I KNOW WHO TO BLAME
FOR THIS OUTRAGE, HICCUP, IT'S YOUR
RIDICULOUS LITTLE AMOEBA OF A DRAGON,
FOOTLESS!'

He pointed at Toothless, who was sitting, giggling, on the remains of the throne.

'He's called *Toothless*, Father,' Hiccup said, hurriedly, 'and I don't think it *was* him, you know, it was probably just a spark from the fire...'

Unfortunately Toothless chose this particular moment to let out a large woody belch, and two great black puffs of smoke shot out of his nostrils, showering them all with throne splinters.

'WHAT DO YOU THINK I AM – *STUPID?*' bellowed Stoick.

'No, no,' murmured Fishlegs, soothingly, 'just a little challenged in the brain cell department... it's traditional in a Viking Chief...'

'SHUDDUP!' roared Stoick, grabbing one of the throne legs and waving it at Hiccup. 'LOOK AT THIS! GUM-MARKS! THAT RIDICULOUS FROG OF YOURS HAS CROSSED THE LINE ONCE TOO OFTEN!'

'I'm sorry, Father...' Hiccup mumbled, miserably. 'Toothless!' he scolded his pet. 'You know you're not supposed to touch anything that belongs to my father.'

'W-w-was WOOD!' Toothless pointed out. 'Hiccup says eat up your wood, so Toothless EAT UP

49

the w-w-wood!'

'I meant the DRIFTWOOD on your plate, and you know it, Toothless,' scolded Hiccup. 'Not the throne.'

Stoick turned from red to purple as a bruise. His voice when he spoke now, was dangerously, carefully calm. 'Hiccup... you weren't talking to your dragon in Dragonese, now, were you?'

'Um... yes, Father... I mean – no, Father...' stammered Hiccup, 'I mean, I don't know, Father...'

'You WERE speaking in Dragonese,' said Stoick. He took a small, stained notebook from out of his pocket. *A Hero's Guide to Deadly Dragons* was written on the front in inky letters. 'And what is this, that I found in your bedroom? Did YOU write this in this notebook, Hiccup?'

'Yes,' admitted Hiccup.

(It was a bit difficult to deny it, as it said *by Hiccup Horrendous Haddock III* underneath the title.) Hiccup had been filling it with descriptions of all the different species of dragons, and the beginnings of a Dragonese Dictionary.

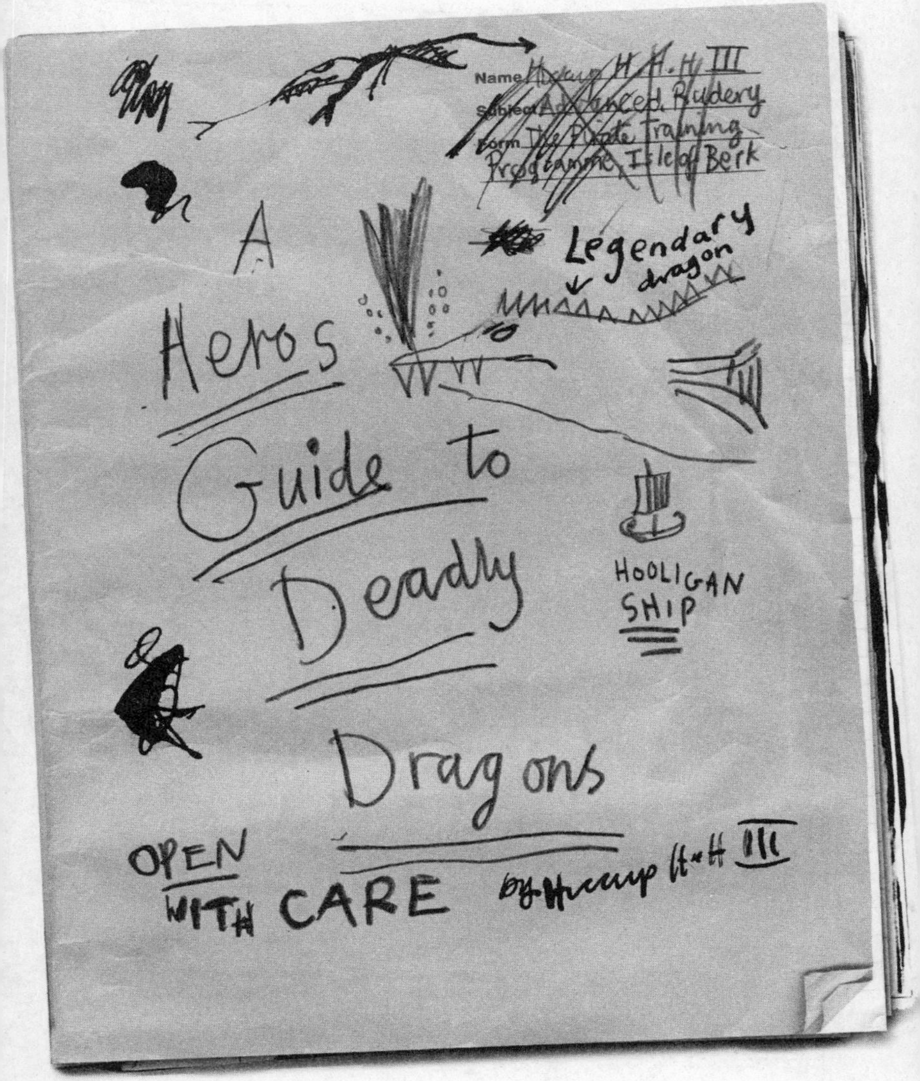

Name
Subject
Form
Programme, Isle of Berk
A Heros Guide to Deadly Dragons
Legendary dragon
HOOLIGAN SHIP
OPEN WITH CARE
by Hiccup H. H. III

Adranced Rudery

Insults that always work well are ones that suggest your enemy is wledy eg. ✔

You have arms as limp as a lettuce and you could not beat a jellyfish in one-to-one combat. DO NOT TRY THIS INSULT on a member of the Murderous Tribe, they may kill you

✔ Nine tri, Hiccup but yoo reely need to work on yoor Badd Sppeling. A troo Hooligan canot spel for toffee, G.B.

'A Hero~~sonous~~ to Deadly ~~are the~~ ~~ons~~.

All dragons are deadly but some are deadlier than others. I will begin with some of my favourites,

THE POISONOUS SPECIES

1. Toxic Nightshades

Toxic nightshades only come out after dark. They are so deadly that they have no natural predators, and they are therefore a very bright luminous yellow. ~~e defeated by~~

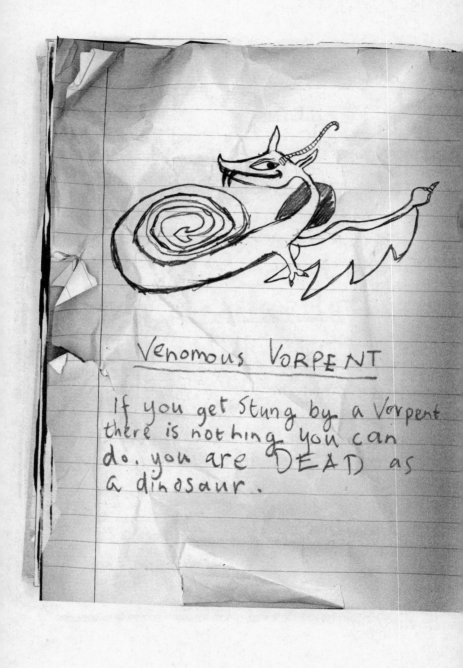

Venomous VORPENT

If you get stung by a Vorpent there is nothing you can do. you are DEAD as a dinosaur.

Poisonous Piffleworms

The bite of a Piffleworm is so deadly that you will be killed in a quarter of a second.

Piffleworms, however, cannot stand the sound of whistling, and they freeze like statues when they hear this noise I found this out one day at Wild Dragon Cliff.

I hatched a single Squirrelserpent make a whole nest of Piffleworms freeze,

HAND

DOWN WITh DOGSBREATH !
UGh UGh UGh!

Toothless

#icup RULES OK

Stoick swelled up furiously, his nostrils flaring like a bull in a bad mood.

This was too much.

'BOOKS! *My* Heir, writing *BOOKS*??' fumed Stoick the Vast. 'You are *supposed* to be a VIKING, Hiccup! THE HORRENDOUS HADDOCKS DO NOT WRITE *BOOKS*! Your terrifying Hooligan ancestors would be turning in their graves! WHAT do Horrendous Haddocks not do, Hiccup?'

Hiccup hung his head.

'Horrendous Haddocks do not write books,' muttered Hiccup, looking at the floor.

'Horrendous Haddocks do not even READ books,' added Stoick. 'Books are banned. Completely. By order of "The Thing"*, as you would know, if you'd been concentrating.

'YOUR LAST REPORT WAS A DISGRACE, HICCUP!' stormed Stoick the Vast. 'YOU SHOULD BE PAYING MORE ATTENTION TO YOUR SENSELESS VIOLENCE! YOUR SHEEP-RUSTLING! NOT DRIFTING AROUND SCRIBBLING AWAY IN *BOOKS*!!!'

Stoick the Vast was so annoyed he was practically levitating in the air. 'BOOKS!!' he snorted furiously. 'BOOKS ARE *USELESS*, HICCUP, *USELESS*.

---

* 'The Thing' was a Meeting of all the local Viking Tribes

THERE IS ONLY ONE BOOK WORTH READING, ONE BOOK THAT IS THE EXCEPTION TO THIS RULE, AND THAT IS *HOW TO TRAIN YOUR DRAGON*, BY PROFESSOR YOBBISH. THAT IS THE ONLY BOOK FOR HOOLIGANS.'

Stoick stopped mid-shout.

He was suddenly struck by a Brilliant Idea – and he didn't get many of *those*.

'In fact, that book's lying around here somewhere, I know it is... Gobber the Belch STOLE that book HIMSELF!'

Books were despised by the Viking Tribes, as they were seen as a horrible civilising influence, and a threat to barbarian culture. Because they were banned they were locked up in the great grim Meathead Public Library, guarded by the terrible Hairy Scary Librarian and his dreadful army of Meathead Warriors and Driller-Dragons.

So scary was this Librarian, that stealing one of these despised books from the Library had become a challenge to the bravest Viking Warriors, and very few could say they had succeeded in the attempt.

'I *wonder*?' Stoick scratched his beard thoughtfully with the throne leg. 'All I have to do is

find that book… show it to Bertha… and that'll
PROVE that Hooligans are just as good at Burglary
as Bog-Burglars! I bet none of Bertha's Warriors have
snaffled a book from right under the nose of the Hairy
Scary Librarian! HEH HEH HEH! The bet is mine,
all *mine*!'

Stoick rubbed his hands together in delighted
glee, chucked the throne leg in the fire – and then
remembered he was still supposed to be telling
Hiccup off.

'Oh, ahem,' said Stoick, hurriedly putting his
stern voice on again, for he was now in a big rush to
go and find the *How to Train Your Dragon* book, 'I am
still very concerned, Hiccup. I am going to get rid of
this silly Deadly Dragon Whatimy book that you've
been writing, and I don't want to hear you speaking
Dragonese, or doing any of this book-writing nonsense
EVER AGAIN.' Stoick stuffed Hiccup's notebook
back in his own breast pocket. 'I want you to start
acting like a future Viking Chief… concentrate on your
Rudery and your Axe-work… stop being friends with
these unsuitable marsh-meddlers,' (he glowered at
Camicazi, who grinned back at him happily) 'and I am
warning you, MOST SERIOUSLY,' (Stoick lowered
his voice to its MOST SERIOUS level) 'if that dragon

of yours does ONE more thing like this… just *one* more thing… I'll… I'll… I'll…'

Stoick racked his brain for a really good punishment.

'I'll BANISH him,' said Stoick finally.

'You wouldn't!' gasped Hiccup in horror.

'I *would*, and I *will*,' said Stoick, firmly. 'You are twelve years old today, Hiccup, so it is time for you to stop messing about and start growing into a proper Viking Hero. It's for your own good.

'Now, *where* did I put that *How to Train Your Dragon* book?' wondered Stoick to himself. 'Ooh, I can't wait to see Big-Boobied Bertha's face when she realises I've won the bet! *That'll* wipe the smirk off those Boobies of hers…'

And Stoick positively skipped out of the room, on his way to the Great Hall to look for it.

'N-n-not a nice man, your father,' huffed Toothless, as Hiccup rubbed the spinach off his back with the tip of his waistcoat. 'He gets v-v-very cross. Me not a ridiculous frog.'

'Well if you WILL go around eating people's thrones, they are going to get cross,' Hiccup scolded Toothless. 'Now, Toothless, I want you to THINK. He really really means it, now. ONE MORE THING and you are out on your ear. Can you think of anything else you might have done that will get us into trouble?'

Toothless looked up at Hiccup with puppy-dog eyes. 'Who – m-m-me?' he said innocently. He shook his head so hard his horns wobbled. 'No way, n-n-not me...'

'Oh, good,' Hiccup said, relieved.

Toothless thought a bit more. He scratched behind his ear thoughtfully, and then began to lick the spinach off his hind leg with his forked tongue. 'W-w-well...' he admitted casually between licks, 'there m-m-might be just one t-t-tiny thing...'

'WHAT tiny thing?' Hiccup asked, his heart sinking.

Toothless sighed and stopped licking for a second. He pointed with one claw towards a large broom resting against the wall in the corner.

Hiccup followed the direction of his claw.

And then he let out a yell his father would have been proud of.

There, hidden behind the broom, were the scattered remains of a book – the burned-out, stomped-on and chewed-over remains of a book with golden clasps and fancy gilt lettering and an unusually thick cover...

... a cover that was torn in half, and ripped
to shreds with sharp little claws, and smeared with
spinach-coloured stripes and now read:

HO* (shred) **TO **AIN Y**R DRAG**** (rip)

4. BOG-BURGLARS DO NOT ALWAYS TELL THE TRUTH

'The Hooligans WORSHIP this stupid book,' Hiccup moaned, picking up one of the torn bits and trying to fit it to another. 'They think it has the answer to everything... My father thinks it's going to win him his bet against Big-Boobied Bertha and NOW look at it... it's *ruined*... what *were* you thinking of, Toothless?'

'W-w-was on the chair,' sniffed Toothless. 'P-p-paper is kind of woody... Me eat the book first, then the chair.'

'What are we going to *do*?' Hiccup wailed, throwing down the bits of book in despair. 'We can't mend this! And Toothless will be banished!'

'Toothless d-d-doesn't want to be banished...' wailed Toothless.

Camicazi was doing a handstand against the wall, but she came down to say, 'I'm sure there's other copies of that book in the Meathead Public Library. All we have to do is nip over there and steal one.'

There was a stunned silence.

'That's a GREAT idea, that is,' said Fishlegs, sarcastically. 'What about the Hairy Scary Librarian and his Heart-Slicers?'

'Oh, come on, it's just one teeny little mad old Librarian guarding that whopping great Library, we could be in and out before he even knew we were there,' said Camicazi breezily. 'How about it, Hiccup? Are you on for proving that Hooligans are just as good at Burglary as Bog-Burglars?'

Now, Camicazi wasn't strictly telling the truth, was she, when she said that the Hairy Scary Librarian was the ONLY person guarding the Meathead Public Library. As we saw in Chapter One, there was also the small matter of the four hundred Meathead Warrior Guards, not to mention their Driller-Dragons.

Unfortunately Hiccup didn't know anything about the Meathead Public Library, apart from the fact that he had met the Hairy Scary Librarian once or twice and he didn't like the look of him. And, he thought, if the Library was as big as Camicazi said it was, perhaps they could just sneak in very quietly and whip one of the books without anyone being any the wiser? And then Toothless wouldn't be banished, and Stoick would be pleased, and they would win his bet for him.

So he said slowly, 'OK then... let's do that...'

And from that moment on, they were DOOMED.

'YIPPEEEE!' sang Camicazi, punching the air. 'It's BURGLARY time! This is great, I've been looking for an excuse to steal my mother's Stealth Dragon!' and she hurried out of the house and towards the Dragon Stables, followed closely by a worried Hiccup, a worried Toothless, and an even more worried Fishlegs.

'Hang on a second,' puffed Hiccup, feeling that the situation was spiralling out of control, 'what's all this about stealing people's Stealth Dragons? What *is* a Stealth Dragon? And where did your mother get it from in the first place?'

'She nicked it from Madguts the Murderous two days ago,' explained Camicazi. 'It's one of their Secret Weapons. I expect that's why she accepted your father's burglary bet. She knew he would NEVER come up with anything more impressive than burgling a Secret Weapon from the Murderous Tribe.'

'Or anything CRAZIER,' Hiccup pointed out, 'NOBODY steals things from Madguts the Murderous... And what are we going to need this Stealth Dragon thing *for*, anyway, if this Library is only guarded by one person?'

'Oh, well,' replied Camicazi, thinking on her feet, 'you never know, the Hairy Scary Librarian could be looking out the window when we turn up... and he won't see us coming, will he, if we're sitting on the back of a Stealth Dragon? Here we are!' she said happily.

Camicazi had now reached the Dragon Stables, and she flung open a particularly enormous stable door, and gestured in triumph to the inside. 'Feast your eyes on that!' whooped Camicazi. '*THAT* is a Stealth Dragon!'

WOW!

THAT. is a Stealth Dragon!

Author's note:
Unfortunately we cannot show you a picture of a Stealth Dragon, due to the fact that they are invisible.

66

5. THE STEALTH DRAGON

At first sight, there appeared to be nothing at all in the stable.

Stealth Dragons are chameleons, which means that they turn exactly the same colour as the background around them. And they are particularly good at it, so good that, even as large as they are, their camouflage makes them practically invisible. Which means that they can sneak up on a Village, or indeed, a Library, without anyone realising they are there.

It took a few seconds for their eyes to adjust and to see the faint ghostly outline of a very large, sleeping dragon, the bottom of it exactly the colour and texture of the pile of hay he was sleeping on, the top just precisely the pattern of the wood he was leaning against, knot-holes and all.

'Isn't this just the coolest thing you ever saw?' sang Camicazi excitedly, running her fingers along the creature's invisible side. 'I've always wanted to ride one of these things!'

'WOW,' breathed Hiccup admiringly. 'WOW, WOW, WOW, WOW, WOW, WOW. Look at its tail spines, they're gigantic... But we can't possibly steal this dragon, Camicazi.'

'Why not?' asked Camicazi, vaulting on to the dragon-shaped block of air that seemed to be the Stealth Dragon's back, waking it up with a start.

'Why not?' squeaked Fishlegs. '*Why not???* This isn't just any old riding-dragon, this is a *Secret Military Weapon*! Madguts the Murderous and those scary Warriors in his Tribe are going to be turning over every stone in the Archipelago looking for this dragon! And *I* don't want to be sitting on its back when they find it!'

'Well, whether you lot come with me or not, *I'm* going to steal this dragon, and pilfer that book, and be back in time for tea,' said Camicazi, doing up the seatbelt on the saddle, and gathering the Stealth Dragon's reins in her hands. 'What are you Hooligans made of?' she said teasingly. 'You're not AFRAID, are you?'

Of course Hiccup was not going to admit that he was afraid to a small blonde girl a whole head shorter than he was.

'I know I'm going to regret this,' said Hiccup, climbing on to the shimmering mirage of the Stealth Dragon.

'Not half as much as I'M going to regret it,' said Fishlegs between gritted teeth, jumping from foot to foot in his anxiety. 'What if Madguts CATCHES us?

He's only the scariest Chief in the entire barbarian world…'

'He *can't* catch us, that's the whole point,' grinned Camicazi, 'because we'll be riding on the back of an invisible dragon, and invisible dragons are un-trackable, that's what makes them such great Secret Weapons. Stop worrying for once in your life, Fishlegs, and get up here and live a little!'

Fishlegs sighed, and followed Hiccup on to the Stealth Dragon's back and the two boys fastened themselves into the seatbelts on the saddle.

The Stealth Dragon's tall, aerodynamically curved back-spines soared up on either side of them, so that they were now as invisible to any onlookers as the Stealth Dragon himself.

'Could we possibly go to the Meathead Public Library? It's just to the right of the Meathead Islands, on a small island called Forget Me?' Hiccup asked the Stealth Dragon politely.

If anybody knows how to train a dragon, it's the Murderous Tribe, and the Stealth Dragon stood to attention and answered with military promptness. 'Absolutely, SIR! Anything you say, SIR! Will that be all, SIR?'

'What a goody-goody,' muttered Toothless.

'And… off… we… GO!' yelled Camicazi, giving the reins a wild shake. 'YOOOICKS!'

The Stealth Dragon leapt into the air the moment the command left her throat. And once Hiccup had caught his breath and begun to peer over the edge of the Stealth Dragon's back fins, the dragon was flying so fast that Berk was a pale purple shadow far behind them, and they were halfway to the Meathead Islands already.

'Will you look at the ACCELERATION on this thing? WAHOOOOOO!' whooped Camicazi above the roaring wind. 'You've got to admit, Fishlegs, this is a ride of a lifetime!'

But Fishlegs was too busy concentrating on not getting dragon-sick to admit to anything of the sort.

Toothless held on to Hiccup's shoulder like a disgruntled robin, his ears flapping in the wind, muttering, 'Us d-d-don't HAVE to go so f-f-fast… don't HAVE to… this g-g-guy he's j-j-just *showing off*…' – as if he had never shown off in his life before.

Stealth Dragons do fly fast.

They fly so fast that by the time they caught sight of the Library itself and Hiccup had realised that Camicazi had not told the truth about the Hairy Scary Librarian being the only guard, and that the place was

in fact absolutely crawling with hundreds of heavily armed Meathead Guards and their Driller-Dragons. By *this* time... it was TOO LATE.

The Stealth Dragon had already sailed sheer over the blackened battlements, as quiet as a whisper.

The invisible creature then hovered next to a window three hundred feet up the Main Library Building, and one by one the Vikings crawled across his invisible wings and on to the window ledge.

Hiccup whispered to the Stealth Dragon to hang about and wait for their return, and the dragon nodded obediently.

'Absolutely, SIR! No problem, SIR! All you have to do is call, SIR!' the dragon whispered back, and he drew back to hover a respectful little distance away.

Camicazi was the first to crawl through the Library window, followed by Fishlegs and then Toothless, so that only Hiccup remained, standing on the tiny, crumbly window ledge.

There he stood for a few seconds, until his attention was momentarily distracted by a passing wild dragon called a Lesser-Spotted Squirrelserpent, and he lost concentration, and slipped off the edge of the window with a shriek.

71

And this is how Hiccup was left hanging at the end of Chapter One.

Only five hours after he woke up on his twelfth birthday, Hiccup found himself dangling by one hand from a window ledge, three hundred feet up in the air, with the Meathead Warrior Guards down below fitting their silver-tipped arrows to their  Northbows, and bending down to let their Driller-Dragons off their chains.

6. WELCOME TO THE MEATHEAD PUBLIC LIBRARY

'EEEEAAAARGH!' screamed Hiccup Horrendous Haddock the Third, swinging violently this way and that, trying to get his other hand back on the ledge. 'STEALTH DRAGON! HELP ME!'

The Stealth Dragon would have been happy to help out. Unfortunately, however, it did not hear Hiccup's desperate cries. It, too, had caught sight of the Lesser Squirrelserpent, and it hadn't eaten since the previous evening.

Appetite had won out over military discipline, and the Stealth Dragon was already a hundred metres away, swooping after the unfortunate Squirrelserpent like a sparrowhawk after a mouse.

zzZZZZZING

A wickedly sharp Northbow arrow narrowly missed taking off the tip of Hiccup's nose.

zzZZZZZING-THUNK!
zzZZZZZING-THUNK!

Two more wickedly sharp Northbow arrows plunged deep into the backpack slung over Hiccup's shoulder.

Released from their chains, the snarling
Driller-Dragons spread their black wings and leapt into
the air, the drills on the ends of their noses viciously
whirring, flying swiftly upward towards where the boy
was hanging.

Two pairs of hands closed over Hiccup's
wrist, and Camicazi and Fishlegs, who
were now kneeling on the window
ledge, hauled him upwards
with a strength they did not
know they had, through
a hail of arrows.

They were
only just in
time.

As they dragged him through the window and into the Library, the drill of the Leading Driller-Dragon just missed the back of Hiccup's heels. The Dragon howled in fury, for the window was too small for it to enter.

'Oh, thank Thor you're safe,' panted Camicazi as they all now stood inside in the gloom of the Library, while the Driller-Dragons revved up their drills to an excruciating whine and screamed in frustrated fury outside.

'You call this *safe*?' coughed Fishlegs, sarcastically.

'AAAAARRRRGGGGGHHHHH!' screamed Hiccup, Fishlegs, Camicazi and Toothless, falling back as a terrifying six-foot-long drill, sharp and spinning, sliced through the air between the four of them.

The Leading Driller-Dragon was not going to be defeated.

In a blinding rage it had thrown itself at the window, cracking it wider so that it could shove its gigantic head and one outstretched arm through the opening.

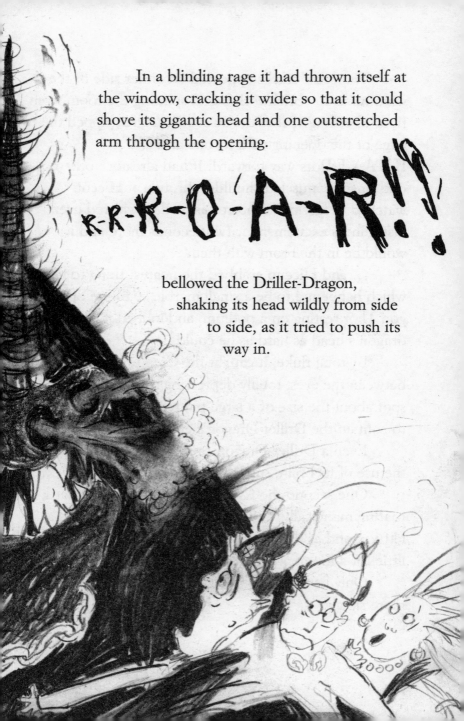

R-R-R-O-A-R!!

bellowed the Driller-Dragon, shaking its head wildly from side to side, as it tried to push its way in.

Two great cracks appeared on either side of the window, as the brickwork burst, splitting the room from floor to ceiling... the Monstrous Creature gripped the edge of the opening with its one arm and H-E-A-V-E-D its way forward. It had already worked one gigantic muscled shoulder through... Hiccup watched in fascinated horror as its drill whirred even faster in its excitement... two seconds more and it would be in the room with them...

... and Hiccup grabbed the nearest thing to hand, which happened to be a small marble statuette of the god Thor resting on a podium, and lobbed it at the dragon's head as hard as he could.

By total fluke, it caught the Creature right between the eyes, totally depressing and wiping out a spot about the size of a large pimple that just happened to contain the Driller-Dragon's entire brain.

Even a Driller-Dragon cannot function without the use of its brain, small as that brain might be.

One second the Creature was plunging forward, roaring maniacally. The next it collapsed, as limp as a lettuce, and as dead as a dinosaur, its limbs jerking a little for a moment, and then going still.

Only its drill continued to whir, but more and more slowly.

The three Vikings and one small dragon stood stock-still in the now quiet, darkened Library, great clouds of dust billowing up around them and beginning to settle down again on the floor.

The drill whirled slower... and slower... and slower... and finally stopped.

'OK, then,' whispered Camicazi shakily, 'so NOW we're safe...'

'Safe? *Safe????*' panted Fishlegs, furiously. '*Safe* would be if we were putting our feet up back on Berk... which is where we *SHOULD* be if we hadn't listened to your CRAZY idea in the first place. In what possible way could you call the situation we find ourselves in now as SAFE?'

'Oh you *boys*,' shrugged Camicazi, 'you're such *worriers*. All we have to do NOW is, find the book, pilfer it, scarper back here again, climb out the window, call up the old Stealth Dragon, and fly back home to Berk. Trust me, Fishlegs, it's no problemo, watch and learn, my boy, watch and learn.'

'No problemo?' raged Fishlegs. '*No problemo?* OK then, Little Miss "We'll Be Back in Time for Tea", just exactly how are we supposed to climb out this window now that Bird-brain here is *jammed right in it?*'

He flung out his arm to indicate the dead

Driller-Dragon, who was, indeed, stuck so tightly into that window, he could have been wearing it as a pair of trousers.

'Ah,' said Camicazi, thoughtfully.

'And that's the *only* window,' Fishlegs pointed out.

'We'll just have to walk out the front door, then,' said Camicazi defiantly.

'Would that be the same front door which, even at this very moment, Meathead Warriors and their Driller-Dragons are pouring through in their HUNDREDS, looking for us? In their HUNDREDS, when you said that this Library was only guarded by ONE small, mad Librarian?' asked Fishlegs politely through gritted teeth.

'I didn't think you would come if you had thought there was more than one guard,' Camicazi pointed out, reasonably.

'Not coming would have been a Very Good Idea!' howled Fishlegs.

Something caught Fishlegs's eye and he turned even whiter than he was already, attempting to climb a nearby column in his anxiety. 'Look!' gasped Fishlegs, nodding in the direction of the ground with a jerk of his head. 'The floor! It seems to be m-m-moving!'

The pattern on the floor was indeed moving, in a

sinuous, writhing wriggle that was almost hypnotic to look at.

'Oh that,' said Camicazi carelessly, '*that's* just the Red Hot Itchyworms that are alarming the floor.'

'*Red Hot Itchyworms!*' squeaked Fishlegs, attempting to climb even higher up the column he was clutching.

Red Hot Itchyworms are tiny little maggot-like dragons that bite considerably harder than either ants or wasps.

'It's all right,' said Hiccup reassuringly, taking a good look at the Itchyworms. 'As long as we're wearing dragonskin shoes, they won't attack us. But you can't touch the floor with anything unprotected... they can bite through ordinary material, and once they get a taste of your blood they'll swarm all over you. I mean, you might have WARNED us, Camicazi!' Hiccup tut-tutted in exasperation.

'FUSSPOTS!' snorted Camicazi.

Fishlegs climbed down from the column and put his dragonskin shoes gingerly on the floor.

'And this is another small point,' Fishlegs grumbled, 'I don't know if you've noticed, but this Library seems to be like some sort of MAZE. How are we going to find our way through it without getting lost?'

'Oh I've thought of that,' replied Camicazi, more confidently this time. 'We're going to follow the Stormfly. The Stormfly *never* gets lost.'

She took her backpack off her shoulders, reached inside, and carefully removed Something from it.

The Something was a hunting dragon the colour of a shiny golden coin.

'Is that *your* dragon?' Hiccup asked. 'I didn't even know you HAD a dragon.'

'*Everybody* has a dragon,' replied Camicazi, rather surprised. 'But mine is independent – we don't need to hang out together the whole time like you guys. Wake up now, Stormfly, I need you...'

She tickled the golden dragon behind its ears to wake it up, which it did with a sort of miaowy sneeze, and Camicazi just pulled her hand away before it nipped her.

Two seconds later and the little dragon was wide awake, curling round Camicazi's ankles, and then up on to her shoulders in such a restless golden streak of quickness that Hiccup couldn't make out its species.

'It's a beautiful dragon,' Hiccup said, 'but what kind is it?'

Hiccup knew the answer before he had finished the question, because on hearing itself called 'beautiful'

the scales of the dragon
blushed from gold to
rose to scarlet like an
instant sunset.

'A MOOD-
DRAGON!' Hiccup
exclaimed in
astonishment.

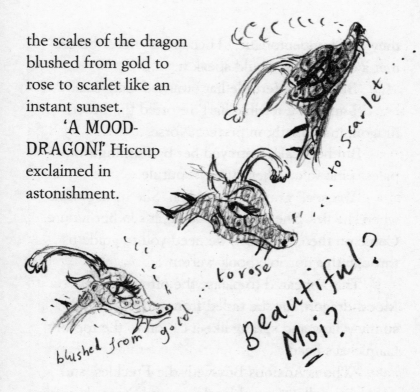

to scarlet....

to rose

blushed from gold

Beautiful? Moi?

'But that's incredibly rare, I've never
seen a Mood-dragon before…'

'Mood-dragons, rare?' snorted Camicazi. 'That's
nothing. *This* is a Mood-dragon that speaks Norse.'

Now, this took Hiccup's breath away.

Long ago, the bards say, dragons and men spoke
together as happily as you or I. Now, Hiccup was one
of the only people he knew who spoke Dragonese, and
although dragons generally understand Norse (which

they call 'lumpentongue') Hiccup had never before met a dragon who could speak it.

'But she's a terrible liar,' warned Camicazi.

'I am not a terrible liar!' retorted the Mood-dragon, indignantly, in perfect Norse.

But her scales betrayed her by flushing from palest pink to a rather pungent purple.

'You see!' grinned Camicazi. 'She turns purple when she lies. She can't help lying, it's in her nature. Come on then, Stormfly, we need you to guide us through this horrible book-warren...'

This appeared to please the offended little Mood-dragon, for she faded from purple into sunny yellow and sprang like a cat on to the top of Camicazi's head.

'Who is Anxious-Boy-with-the-Freckles, and who is my fellow greenblood?' purred Stormfly softly, looking down at Toothless through laughing yellow eyes.

Toothless was acting rather weirdly. He had gone pink around the horns, and he was staring ahead, glassy-eyed, as if stuffed.

He answered gruffly, 'That's Hiccup and me T-t-toothless. Me a very rare Toothless Daydream. Very r-r-rare and very vicious.'

'Hello, T-t-toothless,' admired Stormfly, delicately swishing her yellow tail. 'Oooh, you do look vicious...Viciously handsome. What smart little wings you have!'

At this, Toothless puffed out his chest, and loop-the-looped with pride. He was so busy showing off, he didn't even notice Stormfly's naughty smiling face turning slowly from yellow to purple.

'This still doesn't solve the problem of what we do once we find the book,' said Fishlegs, stubbornly sticking to his gloomy view of the prospect ahead of them.

'Well,' said Hiccup, 'we can either sit here getting depressed, *or* we can go and try and find a copy of *How to Train Your Dragon* by this Professor Yobbish person, and hope we think of something along the way. Whatever we do, it's clear from this point that there is NO GOING BACK.'

This was a good point.

'OK, Stormfly,' said Camicazi, 'take us to the Animal Training section...'

Stormfly took an elegant sniff of the stuffy Library air. Her dainty little nose wrinkled in disgust. 'Left,' announced Stormfly, and Camicazi immediately turned right.

'Erm... you have to do the opposite of what she says,' explained Camicazi.

'Great!' smiled Fishlegs, sarcastically. 'Our trusty guide through this maze of Death is a pathological liar! It doesn't get better than this, really...'

'OH, stop being so GLOOMY about everything, Fishlegs,' said Camicazi, breezily. 'It's always all right in the end... Thor only knows how...'

So Hiccup and Fishlegs set off into the dark, tangled heart of the Library, tiptoeing after Camicazi and Stormfly through the long twisty corridors, with Toothless flapping at the rear.

Toothless
was acting
rather
weirdly...

7. HIGH IN THE MURDEROUS MOUNTAINS

Fishlegs would have felt gloomier still if he could have seen what was happening high in the sinister crags of the Murderous Mountains, where the Murderous Tribe had their hide-out.

The Murderous Tribe did not often receive visitors. Perhaps it was their uncomfortable habit of sacrificing intruders to the Sky Dragons at the point of Mount Murderous that kept people at bay. Or maybe it was their SMELL.

They lived on a repellent diet of month-old rotten haddock stuffed with pickled onions and bad eggs, all washed down with enormous quantities of BEER, which, as you can imagine, would make *anybody* pong a bit after a while.

Whatever the reason, the Murderous Tribe were generally left to enjoy the peace and quiet of their sinister mountaintop home. And such was their reputation, nobody came in a friendly way to nick their sheep, or burgle their reindeer, in that neighbourly, Viking-ly manner that was the fashion all over the rest of the Archipelago.

sniff SNIFF

So Bertha's cheeky burglary of Madguts's newest military weapon took them entirely by surprise.

Madguts's henchman, Gumboil, knelt in the dust before the open stable door, peering at the muddle of footprints, and poking at the soil with one black-gloved finger. He was joined in this exercise by five gigantic Sniffer Dragons, their enormous nostrils pushing through the dirt like bloodhounds as they searched for a scent.

Gumboil was carrying Madguts's terrifying arsenal.

Fifty Murderous Warriors, and Madguts himself, were watching Gumboil poke. 'Stolen!' Gumboil hissed in disbelief. 'By the Beard of Great Stinking Hairy-Knuckled Thor, Your Violence's Stealth Dragon has been STOLEN!'

One of the scariest things about Madguts the Murderous was that he never spoke.

Nobody quite knew why. Some say he had no tongue, and others say he had lost his voice-box, but whatever might be the reason, he was never heard to do anything more than grunt. He grunted now.

Gumboil leapt sycophantically to his feet and stood on his tiptoes as Madguts grunted furiously into his oily ear.

'Chief Murderous is VERY ANNOYED,' spat Gumboil at the silent Murderous Warriors gathered all around. 'He orders you to track down the perpetrator of this outrage before nightfall, or he will be selling the lot of you to the Ugli-thug Slavelands!'

There was an excited hiss and bark, and a swish of forked tails from the Sniffers as they finally picked up the scent of the stolen Stealth Dragon. 'After them!' yelled Gumboil, running to mount his own dragon.

'And by the orders of his Viciousness, Madguts himself, the one that catches the burglar red-handed shall have extra rotten eggs with his haddock tonight!'

The Murderous Tribe raced to their dragons, and they took off after the Sniffers towards the east, and the distant silhouette of the little Isle of Forget Me.

The Murderous Tribe did not often receive visitors

8. NO GOING BACK

The only window in the Library was now plugged by one fat, dead Driller-Dragon, and no natural daylight could sneak its way into the gigantic, endless maze. The walls were lined with books. Thousands and thousands of bookcases stretched from floor to ceiling, lit only by the dim light of Glow-worms, clinging to the walls, and a faint scarlet gleam given off by the wriggling Itchyworms.

Hiccup walked on, shivering not just with cold, but with fear.

For the Library was cold with that dark, damp cold that has not seen daylight for so many years that it has forgotten what sunshine feels like. The sad, soggy rooms smelt of silence and secrets. The Library felt to Hiccup like a poor neglected fishy Creature who nobody remembers had died in some forgotten corner, and was slowly decaying.

And it was SPOOKY. Choking dust clouds filled some of the halls, and in others the Glow-worms had gone out and they were feeling their way through absolute darkness.

In others, the shelves had clearly been attacked by Driller-Dragons.

Way, way in the distance they could hear the faint echoes of shouting Meathead Warriors and their barking Driller-Dragons as they poured into the Library Entrance, beginning their search for the three Viking Intruders. Surely the Library Labyrinth was so huge that the Searchers, even in those numbers, would take a long, long time to find them?

And maybe it was Hiccup's imagination which was jumping about like a poor bird dashing its head against a window pane, but he kept on thinking that he heard strange *breathing* and *snuffling* noises coming from somewhere behind his shoulder.

Sometimes he thought he saw a flicker of shadows moving and disappearing around a blurry corner.

Toothless no longer flew after them. He had crept into Hiccup's furry waistcoat, his back-spines a prickle of fear and alarm. 'Issa not s-s-safe...' he whispered. 'There's B-B-BAD things in here... trust T-t-toothless... Toothless knows...'

Even through his terror, however, Hiccup was blown

93

"WOW..." breathed Hiccup, "if you stayed here long enough you really could find out the answer to EVERYTHING..."

away with excitement at seeing so many books in one place at one time. He had scribbled away in notebooks himself, of course, but because books were banned by order of 'The Thing', the only proper book he had ever really held was that copy of *How to Train Your Dragon* that Toothless had incinerated. And he hadn't been very impressed by that particular book.

Not enough words, in his opinion.

But here, it was like entering a cave full of treasure.

'WOW,' breathed Hiccup, 'if you stayed here long enough you really could find the answer to everything...'

There were fat books, thin books, volume after decaying volume of the *Encyclopedia Barbaria*... Guides to the Archipelago, and to strange, lost, far-away lands that Hiccup had heard spoken of by the bards, with names like jewels – 'Russia', 'China', 'India', 'Africa' and 'Japan'.

Were these places really REAL or as imaginary as the unicorn? Hiccup longed to stop and pull out the dusty maps... Could there really be a land so hot that your thoughts boiled over in the steam of the day, a land where 'elephants' flew over herds of peaceful 'flamingoes', wandering over a world as warm as bread from the oven?

It seemed extremely unlikely, and Hiccup burned to know the answers.

Hiccup burned to know the answers... but he did not stop.

And they were enormously relieved when Camicazi announced triumphantly that they had reached the Dragons and Other Exotic Creatures section of the library.

'Now, who wrote it again, remind me?' asked Camicazi.

'Professor Yobbish,' replied Hiccup.

'It's over here,' said Fishlegs, kneeling in a corner of the hall. 'W... X... Y for Yobbish... Great Gulpings of Thor, he's written a book about keeping SHARKS as pets, what was the man thinking of? *Here* we are! *How to Train Your Dragon!*'

And there it was, the exact replica of the one that had sat in the Hooligan Great Hall for so many years, and that was now hidden under Hiccup's bed, shredded to pieces by Toothless's expert little claws. Well, perhaps not an exact replica.

'It's a second edition,' Fishlegs pointed out.

'No one will notice,' said Hiccup, jubilantly taking it out of Fishlegs's hands and checking that it was all there.

It certainly was: the big handsome cover with the twiddly bits on it, and inside the three, golden, sacred words that were the whole of Yobbish's advice on the subject:

YELL AT IT.

But this time, after twenty years of painstaking research and as this was a second edition, he had added the vital word... LOUDLY.

It may not seem like much, but the Hooligans had been following this advice with awed obedience for generations.

Hiccup stuffed the book into his backpack.

'Just look at all these *incredible* books on dragons!' he exclaimed in excitement. '*Viking Dragons and their Eggs! Dragons of the Icy Depths! Dragons of the Frozen North!* Think how helpful it would be to the Viking Tribes if we were allowed to read all these books...'

'I hate to hurry you,' said Fishlegs, 'but we're in a bit of a tight spot here, remember?'

'You could be right,' said Hiccup. 'I've got this horrible feeling we might be being followed...'

'Why do you think THAT?' squeaked Fishlegs in alarm.

'Oh, it's just a feeling I have...' said Hiccup.

'I could be wrong, of course. Which direction do we have to go in to get out of here, Stormfly?'

'Right,' said the Stormfly.

And Camicazi was just about to turn *left* around the corner… when a tall, thin Something stepped out of the shadows, out of nowhere, and barred the way.

'Silence in the library,' whispered the Something. And with a nasty, screeching scrape the Something drew its Heart-Slicers from their two scabbards, and held them on either side of Camicazi's face.

'Sssssssshhhhh…' whispered the Something.

9. THE HAIRY SCARY LIBRARIAN

The Something was a man as tall and thin as a broom, with a wild mop of hair, and a beard so long he could have wiped his feet on it. He had tucked this beard into his belt, along with a whole armoury of nasty-looking weapons, axes, swords, and the terrifying Northbow.

Hiccup immediately recognised the man as the Hairy Scary Librarian himself, for he had seen him many times before at Elders' Meetings. Somehow, though, he hadn't looked half as scary out in the open air, surrounded by the other Viking Warriors. Here, in the cold heart of his Library, with his cold, sad, half-blind eyes, and his cracked voice whispering like his throat was full of broken glass, *here*, he was very scary indeed.

'The Library is closed,' croaked the Hairy Scary Librarian.

Camicazi backed away from him. 'Umm... yes, we were just leaving, actually...' she said, quietly drawing out her own sword.

'Ssssh...' said the Librarian. 'Your friend has one

99

of my books in his backpack. It is STRICTLY
FORBIDDEN to remove books from the Library. Give
it back to me, please, or I shall be reluctantly forced to
kill you.'

Hiccup drew his sword as well.

(Fishlegs TRIED to draw his, but unfortunately it
stuck in the scabbard, and however hard he tugged, he
couldn't pull it out.)

'I'm very, very sorry,' said Hiccup, politely, and
he meant this most sincerely for Hiccup wasn't a
natural Burglar, 'but I really, really need this book. It's
a matter of life or death.' And then he went on, less
politely, for he was feeling rather indignant about this,
'And these books aren't just YOUR books, they belong
to the whole of the Viking Nations. We should ALL
be allowed to read them, and this really should be a
Library that is open to the Public. All this knowledge
could be very important.'

'Well, I'm very sorry, too,' whispered the Hairy
Scary Librarian, sadly shaking his head and drawing
out another sword with his left hand. 'But I think that
these books are MINE all MINE.' A horrible gloating
and greedy look came into his mad, blind eyes.
'Perhaps you should bring this up with "The Thing"...
However I'm not sure they will listen to you as books

are considered to be DANGEROUS, and strictly banned, by their own order. And furthermore, it will be rather difficult for you to bring it up because you will be **DEAD**.'

And the Librarian lunged at Hiccup with the sword in his right hand, and at Camicazi with the sword in his left, and the three of them began to fight.

'Can't we talk about this, like reasonable people?' asked Hiccup, jumping out of the way of the Librarian's razor-sharp sword, and nipping in with a thrust of his own.

'Did I say I was a reasonable person?' whispered the Librarian in surprise.

'Mash him!' squealed Toothless, who like all dragons, had a bloodthirsty streak, 'Rip him and tear him and stomp on him and bite him and take all his eggs!'

The Librarian was a very fine swordfighter, for both Camicazi and Hiccup were extremely good at swordfighting themselves, and the Librarian was fighting them both at the same time.

'OOOhhhh, you're really quite good at this, for a Moronic Meathead,' exclaimed Camicazi in pleasure, as he deflected her Loki's Lunge with Double Twist, and replied with a Thrusting Thor and a couple of

Swivelling Swipes.

Camicazi loved to have the practice of fighting a really good opponent.

'Be quiet,' hissed the Hairy Scary Librarian. 'Unless you want the Driller-Dragons to find us and death by Driller-Dragon is such an untidy way to **DIE**. Far neater to go swiftly on the point of my Heart-Slicers, but it's up to you, of course…'

Hiccup was in fine form, neatly dodging the Librarian's fiercest sword strokes, and throwing in some challenging thrusts of his own, while Camicazi's sword was swivelling like a tornado.

Toothless and Stormfly also entered into the battle, shrieking rude encouragements, and flying as close as they dared so they could nip in and bite the Librarian on the sword-arm in order to put him off.

But on the other side, the Librarian seemed to be unmoved by the dragon-bites. He was a fully-grown adult, much stronger and bigger than they were, calm and capable as a juggler at fighting both of them at the same time, and every thrust he made was aimed at their hearts.

'You know, I've got a bad feeling about this, Camicazi,' said Hiccup, slightly nervously, as the Librarian deflected his Double-Backed Left-Handed Through-Lunge, 'I think this guy could be a FlashMaster like Humungously Hotshot the Hero.'*

'You know, I was just wondering the very same thing,' said Camicazi, with interest. 'Only a FlashMaster would know how to parry a Switch-hander... an Overpoint... and a Golden Grimpiercer... and live to tell the tale...'

FlashMasters were the very highest of Sword-Artists. They had all studied under the Great Flashburn himself, at his School of Swordfighting, and they were virtually unbeatable at the Art.

'I *is* a FlashMaster,' croaked the Hairy Scary Librarian, and his death mask grin was most horrible to behold, 'and I is going to croak you with me Heart-Slicers... from your goggle-screams...' (The Hairy Scary Librarian lunged to the right at Camicazi's

---

*Please see *How to Twist a Dragon's Tale*

throat, and she *just* managed to turn the blade away in time, so that it only scratched her a little.) '… to your grub-washers…' (The Hairy Scary Librarian lunged to the left at Hiccup's stomach, and Hiccup just managed to bring down his own sword in time, so that he was only given a tiny graze.)

'Fishlegs!' shouted Hiccup, shakily, 'Help! Go and look up in the Swordfighting Section over there, I can see a book by Flashburn and it might say how to defeat a Sword-Artist…'

Fishlegs had been spending the past ten minutes struggling to get his sword out of his scabbard. Now he jumped to the Swordfighting Section, and ran a trembling finger along the 'F' shelf. '… Fiercethrust… Fighthard… Here it is! Flashburn!' He dragged out the big heavy book called *Swordfighting with Style*, and riffled through the pages looking for Sword-Artistry.

The Hairy Scary Librarian was a little confused as to why the fight was still going on. As a great FlashMaster, who had had ten years of personal one-on-one tuition from the world-reknowned Flashburn, swordfights against him normally did not last very long.

All right, so he had two opponents this time, but they were only *children*, one as skinny as a prawn, and the other a tiny little blonde girl. Admittedly they were extraordinarily good swordfighters for children, but still, he should have been standing over their two dead bodies five minutes ago, wiping their blood off his Heart-Slicers with the end of his beard.

'Why is you not croaked yet?' hissed the Hairy Scary Librarian in surprise. 'You is so titchy and so piddly. Is scrambling my brain-boxer that you is not worm-burgers some time ago...'

The Hairy Scary Librarian was still confident of success, however.

He gathered up his strength for the final attack, closed his eyes so that he was totally blind and could better channel energy from the great god Woden... and launched himself outward to the left and right with deadly accuracy.

His Heart-Slicers simultaneously thrust aside the swords of both Hiccup and Camicazi and plunged towards their hearts like heat-seeking missiles...

... and Fishlegs saw the peril of the moment as he flicked desperately through the pages of *Swordfighting with Style* muttering... 'Lunges... Parries... Double Cartwheels... Oh, bother this for a load of lobsters!'

FLASHBURN's Swordfighting with Style

Most Vikings have absolutely NO IDEA how to swordfight. Their idea of a battle is to bonk someone else on the head while making a loud grunting noise. It takes a genius such as myself, Flashburn the Flashmaster, to instruct these poor, ignorant brutes in the delicate art of lunging, parrying and Double-Backed Left-Handed Over-Pointing.

← A portrait of ME, Flashburn the Flashmaster, looking even more handsome, brilliant and dashing than I normally do. Notice my beautiful, curling moustache and my magnificent bulging MUSCLES!

For some reason, I have spent my life being ATTACKED by my fellow Vikings — jealousy, I suppose. This has led me to perfect the art of swordfighting to the very highest level. I am now UTTERLY BRILLIANT at it. I shall try and explain some of simpler moves in such a way that even a hopeless idiot such as yourself can understand what I am talking about.

Basic Moves

1.
The Deadly Dancer
Get those toes a-twinkling.

2.
The old 'Good Gracious, is that a Lesser Spotted Squirrelserpent I can see up there?' trick. Still surprisingly effective.

Wow!

3.
a.   b.   c.

The Flashy Turnover
Make sure your helmet is a snug fitting one.

4.
(This is ... within the ... but it doe...

The Pretending-You-Are-Dead

ALL YOU NEED
SWORDF
... AND

Flashburn's School of Swor...
the only place to go. If you want
how to swordfight. In this handy
you can learn all your swordfighting
without having the trouble of crossing the
dragon hatching grounds

Praise for 'Swordfighting with Style':

'Flashburn is a genius!'
He taught me all I know,
Flashburn the Flashmaster

'He taught me all I know,'
Humungously Hotshot the Hero

And he took a good hold of the heavy
Swordfighting with Style book, and he swung
it as hard as he could at the Hairy Scary
Librarian's head.

The book made contact with a
confident **WHACK!** And the Hairy
Scary Librarian, who was already
a little off balance with those
lunges going to the left and
the right at the same
time, lost his footing
on the Library floor.
His Heart-Slicers
flew up and missed their
targets, with only milliseconds
to spare, and the Hairy Scary
Librarian wobbled on the spot... lost
his balance and fell heavily to the floor...
knocking out Stormfly with the flailing back
of his sword-hand as he went down.

The Hairy Scary Librarian was wearing shin-
length dragonskin Wellington boots, but his backside
was only protected by thin leather trousers. And, if you
remember, the Library floor was alarmed by Red Hot
Itchyworms.

So the instant his bony bottom touched the
ground, the minuscule Itchyworms swarmed in their
trillions and zillions and numberless frillions all over
his Hairy Scary tummy, across his Hairy Scary chest,

up to his Hairy Scary scalp, and streamed
down into his dragonskin shoes.

The Hairy Scary Librarian leapt to his feet as if
electrified.

He knew better than *anyone* how vital it was not
to make any loud noises in the Library. He dropped
his sword, clamped his hands over his mouth, and
went purple in the face in his effort not to laugh.

An attack by Red Hot Itchyworms feels as if
every single nerve-ending in your entire body is being
tickled at exactly the same time.

It is *infinitely* worse than having ants in your
pants. The Hairy Scary Librarian danced wildly from
foot to foot, scratching himself frantically.

'MMMMMFFFFFFFFFFFFFF,' gurgled the Hairy
Scary Librarian. 'MMMMMFFFF.'

The Itchyworms had been making steady
progress down the shoes, and now they got to the soles
of the Hairy Scary Librarian's feet.

The Hairy Scary Librarian lost it.

He forgot about not making a noise.

He forgot about everything.

For the first time in twenty-five years the
Librarian laughed.

'HAHAHAHAHAHAHAHAHA!' roared the

Hairy Scary Librarian.

And then,

'HAHAHEEHEEOHFORTHOR'SSAK
ESTOPITHAAAHHHAAA! HEEEE!'

And then he fled for the exit, for he knew he
had to get out of there, quick. And as he ran, he was,
laughing and itching and screaming hysterically,

'RUN FOR YOUR LIVES! HEE-HEE!
HEAD QUICKLY AND CALMLY
FOR THE EXITS!
NO PUSHING!
NO SHOVING!
HA HA HA
HA HA! EVACUATE
THE LIBRARY!
HAHAHAHA!'

Now, Hiccup and Fishlegs and Camicazi and
Toothless would have done well to have followed him,

and taken his advice.

But they weren't concentrating on the Hairy Scary Librarian.

Camicazi had picked up the stunned, limp body of the Stormfly, and was cradling her in her arms. 'Wake up, you little liar…' whispered Camicazi. 'Come on now… don't do this to me…'

And to Hiccup's astonishment, Toothless, who normally cared for nobody but himself, was practically crying, and licking Stormfly's paw to try to wake her up.

10. BIG, BIG TROUBLE

She had turned completely white... which didn't look hopeful... but after a few minutes the gold slowly began to return to her body again, her lashes trembled, and she finally opened her eyes.

'She's a-a-alive!' yelled Toothless happily, and he did a somersault in the air.

'Oh, thank Thor,' sighed Camicazi. 'How are you feeling?'

'I'm feeling like a dragon who has been hit on the head,' said Stormfly, rubbing the large lump that had appeared between her horns. 'Who are you?'

'What do you mean, who am I?' said Camicazi in surprise. 'I'm Camicazi of course... your Master.'

'And who is the boy who looks like a fish? And what about this skinny red one all covered in freckles? And, most importantly WHO AM I and why...' asked Stormfly, with mounting horror, '...why am I speaking the language of the lumpentongue?'

'You're the Stormfly. You've always spoken Norse,' stammered Camicazi. 'Stop joking around, Stormfly, we're in trouble here...'

'I'm not joking,' said Stormfly.

And to Hiccup's concern, not even a hint of

'Who am I?' asked the Stormfly 'and why am I speaking the language of the lumpentongue?'

violet came over her as she said it.

'What am I doing in this horrible cold dungeon?' asked Stormfly.

'It's a long story,' said Hiccup, hurriedly. 'But the important thing is, can you remember the way OUT of here?'

'Well,' said the Stormfly, rubbing her head again. 'I can't remember how I got IN, so how am I supposed to remember how to get OUT?'

There was a nasty silence, as the three young Vikings suddenly realised exactly how much trouble they were in.

Big, big, BIG trouble.

The Library seemed to have got even darker since the Hairy Scary Librarian had shrieked out of the room. One by one, the Glow-worms were dimming their glows. The loud cries of the Hairy Scary Librarian's hysterical cracked laugh could be heard echoing and twisting down the corridors.

It was as if the Library was laughing at them.

Heh-heh-heh-HEH... smirked the Library.

HEH-HEH-HEH-HEH-HEH...

And another echo was reverberating uncomfortably in Hiccup's brain. It was the echo of the words: 'I'd advise you to be quiet... or the Driller-Dragons will find you... and take it from me, you don't want the Driller-Dragons to find you... It's an untidy way to die...'

Hiccup swallowed hard.

The Library stopped laughing, and now the silence was so loud and so thick you could almost touch it.

Hiccup's anxious, stretching ears strained to hear through the blanket of blackness.

oh, for Thor's sake...

Could that muted snuffle
be the noise of dragons hunting?
Could that gentle patter be the drum of running feet?
And way back in the background, that soft and grim
pulsation, could that whirring whining be the hum of
distant drills?

'OK,' whispered Hiccup, his heart now beating
in an erratic tattoo, but trying to keep his voice calm.
Nobody else seemed to be hearing the noises he was
hearing, and he didn't want to worry the others. 'We'll
just set off then, shall we, and see if it jogs the
Stormfly's memory. Which way first, then, Stormfly?'

'Are you talking to *me*?' asked the Stormfly,
pointing her wing to her chest.

'Yes,' whispered Hiccup. 'You're the Stormfly, that's your name.'

'Nice name, I like it, it's got style,' said the Stormfly, very pleased with herself. 'But I haven't got the foggiest which way to go. Right?'

'So... *should* we go right, then?' said Fishlegs. 'Or left? Do you think the knock on the head has made her more truthful?'

'She still looks gold,' said Hiccup trying to see in the gloom. 'I think we'll go right.'

'This just couldn't be better,' said Fishlegs. 'Now our trusty Guide is not only a pathological liar, but has also lost her memory... Marvellous. Superb. EXCELLENT.'

'Well, it's all your fault,' snapped Camicazi. 'You shouldn't have broken up the fight. We were SLAUGHTERING that guy! We had him just where we wanted him!'

'Exactly where you wanted him?' snorted Fishlegs. 'Exactly where you wanted him? So you WANTED him with his sword running right through you like a Bog-Burglar kebab, did you? Silly me, and there was I thinking I've just saved your life and maybe you could thank me, just a little... but, *oh*, *no*, you WANTED him to be killing you, didn't you...'

'*Will you keep your voices down?*' hissed Hiccup in a panic, starting to follow Stormfly who had begun to flap off to the right. The bonk on her head had affected her flying, and she zigzagged and swayed eccentrically through the air, bumping into things.

'Sorry, sir,' apologised Stormfly, to yet another bookshelf. 'This way, guys, I think my memory could be returning...'

They were all rather encouraged by Stormfly's confidence, despite the fact that she kept on bumping into things. But after about half an hour of running round the Library without seeming to get anywhere at all, that confidence wore off.

'You haven't a clue where we are, have you, Stormfly?' panted Fishlegs.

'Weeell,' said Stormfly, 'it seems to be a big creepy place with loads and loads of BOOKS in it... I give up... is it a school? THIS WAY, GUYS!'

And she doubled up on herself enthusiastically.

'Oh for Thor's sake,' moaned Fishlegs, staggering after the others as they set off again.

Ten minutes later, puffing asthmatically, he called everybody to a halt. 'I've got to rest for a bit...' wheezed poor Fishlegs, 'and we're not really getting anywhere are we?'

'OK,' whispered Hiccup, looking nervously around him. The noises were nearer now, but still the others seemed not to have noticed them. 'We can stop for a moment, and then we have to get on again...'

Fishlegs leaned back on one of the bookcases, panting heavily.

Unfortunately, it was exactly the bookcase that Toothless had chosen to rest on, and in the darkness Fishlegs accidentally poked him in the stomach.

Toothless was not the kind of dragon to suffer in silence.

'EEEEEEOOOOOOW!' shrieked Toothless.

'Sssssshhhhhhhhhhhhhhhh!!!!!' hissed Hiccup.

A loud and thrilling noise came rumbling down the passages of the Library. It began as a low murmur, vibrating through the dragonskin under Hiccup's feet, and then built slowly into a terrifying carnivore ROAR that howled its way down the passages, and through the halls, bouncing off the books and shaking the eardrums of the poor petrified Vikings and their dragons, until the Library echoed around them like a cage of hungry lions.

And now there was no question of what the noise was. It was the sound of a crowd of padding feet, first walking, and then breaking into shuddering springing runs, the noise of DRILLER-DRAGONS stampeding through the Library looking for something to eat, and the sound of their DRILLS whirring round hungrily.

R-R-O-A-R!! grunt.. snuffle... whine...

11. HIDE-AND-SEEK WITH DRILLER-DRAGONS

Camicazi, Hiccup and Fishlegs ran back through the corridors as fleet as foxes with the full cry of the Hunt after them. Down along the twisty tunnels they fled, the Library now a terrifying Babel of screaming and roaring and shouting, all echoing each other in a confusing Pandemonium of noise so loud that it tore at the ears and pierced to their very back-bones.

'Ooooh!' squealed Stormfly happily, 'what are we playing now? Is it Hide-and-Seek? Is it? Is it? I LOVE Hide-and-Seek!'

R-R-R-R-R-

Oooh, can I play?

'We're playing Run-Away-As-Fast-As-You-Can-From-the-Homicidal-Dragon-Monsters...' panted Fishlegs. 'Again! I just cannot believe my bad luck...'

'Up here! It's a short cut!' yelled Camicazi. They scrambled up a rickety ladder, extraordinarily tall, up through a hole in the roof, where they crawled on hands and knees before dropping back down into another corridor again.

-O-A-R!!

They rounded a corner to find a crouching Driller-Dragon, poised to spring. Camicazi screamed, and toppled over a tall tottering bookcase on him.

On and on they ran through the Noise, until Fishlegs came to a panting halt, and gasped, 'I... really... can't... go... any... further...'

'Nor can I,' panted Camicazi, drawing her sword. 'We'll have to stand and fight them.'

'We haven't got a hope of defeating so many,' gasped Hiccup, drawing his sword too.

'Well then,' sang out Camicazi defiantly, the light of battle in her bright blue eyes, 'we shall DIE a Hero's death, FIGHTING TO THE LAST!'

'I *hate* it when you say things like that...' whimpered Fishlegs.

'D-d-d-esert!' shrieked Toothless, 'I think we should desert!'

'Good idea!' approved Hiccup. 'But where to?'

It was a good point.

There was nowhere to go.

'Come on!' shouted Camicazi. 'Help me build a barricade with these books!' And she began pulling books off the shelves, and loading them into a pile by the entrance, as if this pathetic obstacle was going to keep hundreds of hungry Driller-Dragons at bay.

Fishlegs and Toothless helped her, and Stormfly was still thinking that this was a jolly game and kept on knocking the pile over, in fits of giggles, and Hiccup looked around the room they had ended up in, desperately searching for something, *anything*, that he could use to help them in their final, hopeless stand.

And then his eye caught a gleam of dancing brightness.

There it was.

A book on the bookshelf opposite appeared to be GLOWING. All around it was a bright chink of light, as clear as the day.

And as he stepped towards the glowing book, Hiccup gave a gasp of astonished amazement.

His OWN NAME was written on the side of it. HICCUP HORRENDOUS HADDOCK in big golden letters.

Now, there are those who do not believe in Fate.

And there are those that do. But just ask yourself: what are the chances of Hiccup looking around this very room, and his eye alighting on a book with his own name on it? What are the chances of that, I say? Minuscule-y small, and that is why I personally feel that Fate must have led them to that particular room. They had been running through rooms just like this one all day, all lined with bookcases floor to ceiling, and all smelling faintly of fish.

But in this enormous great tangled book-warren of a Library, which must have had thousands and thousands of rooms in it, the room that they had ended up in was the ONLY room that contained a

book written by HICCUP HORRENDOUS
HADDOCK.

'Roaring Razorclams!' exclaimed Hiccup,
lowering his sword, and his jaw dropping. 'This is
EXTRAORDINARY! That book has been written by
someone with exactly the same name as ME!'

Actually, as he drew nearer, he realised it wasn't
EXACTLY the same name. The author was Hiccup
Horrendous Haddock *the Second*.

'I would of course find that fascinating,' moaned
Fishlegs, frantically dragging books off the shelves, as
the sound of drumming feet grew louder and louder,
cutting through the general cacophony of the Noise, 'if
I wasn't just about to DIE, will you come and HELP
US for Thor's sake?'

Hiccup stepped forward towards the books,
as if hypnotised. 'It must be a relative of mine,
a grandfather or something?' whispered Hiccup. 'I
guess if *I'm* the Third, there must have been a First,
and a Second, mustn't there?'

This had never occurred to Hiccup. 'But my
father's never talked about this guy before,' he said
slowly.

In fact, what had he said, only this morning?
'THE HORRENDOUS HADDOCKS DO NOT

WRITE BOOKS. Your Hooligan ancestors would be turning in their graves.'

But his father had not told Hiccup the truth, had he? Here was a Horrendous Haddock who clearly HAD written books. And as Hiccup drew nearer still he almost laughed. It could not be a coincidence, it had to be Fate. There it was, a big, glowing green and gold book called *A Hero's Guide to Deadly Dragons* by Hiccup Horrendous Haddock the Second. It was EXACTLY the same name as the book Hiccup had been writing himself for the last six months, in that scruffy old exercise book that Stoick had confiscated only that morning.

Hiccup pulled out the book, and as it came away from the shelf in a cloud of dust, it left a book-shaped rectangle of bright daylight in the darkness.

A Hero's Guide to Deadly Dragons was the only REAL book on the shelf. The rest were fake, false backs of books, only centimetres deep, stuck to the wood in rows. There was a loud CLICK and smoothly, quietly, the entire bookshelf swung open like a door.

The door stuck a little on the Library floor, and Hiccup dragged it open. And, as he pulled it wider, beautiful bright daylight, and air as fresh as a gulp of water, poured into the room.

The tunnel had not been used for a hundred years, so it was a bit DUSTY.

THE

Dragon-

Whisperer's

Way →

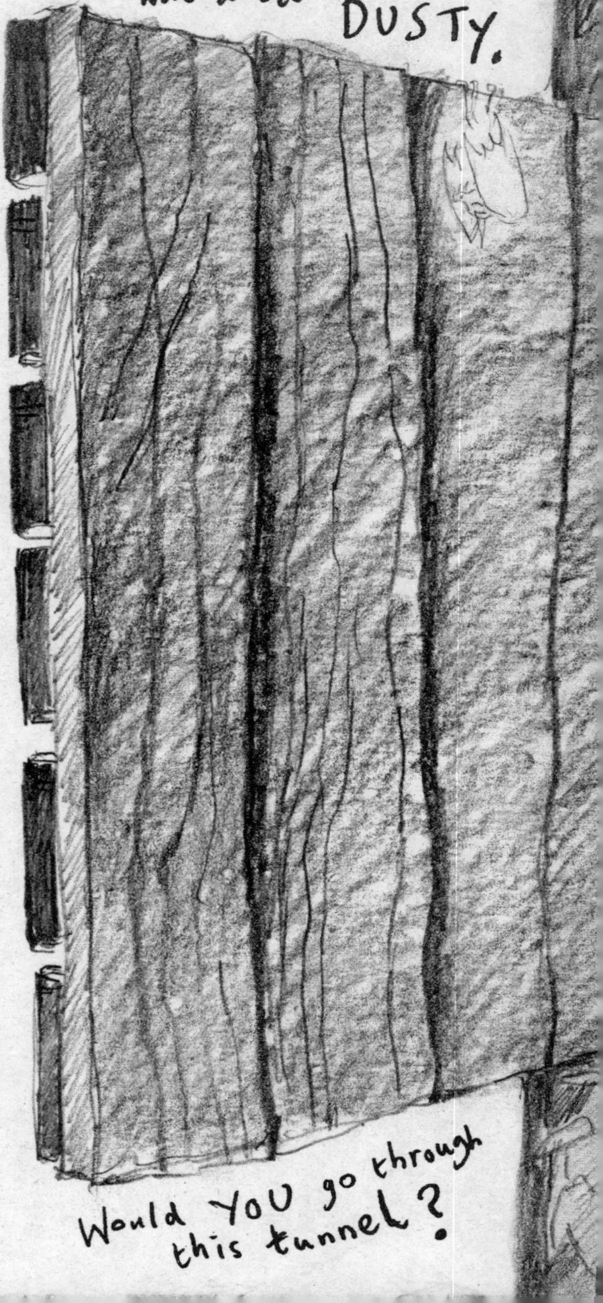

Would YOU go through this tunnel?

Behind that bookshelf door was a short tunnel, and at the end of the tunnel was a glorious blue circle of sky. Scrawled on the inside of the door, were the words, *The Dragon-whisperer's Way*.

Camicazi and Fishlegs stopped their frantic efforts to build a wall out of books, and their jaws flopped downwards in astonishment. Camicazi gave a joyous shout, and ran across the room, intending to climb up into the tunnel.

But Hiccup yelled out in alarm, and drew her back. For, even through the dazzle of the daylight, he could see that the tunnel was not empty. There was a whole heap of sleeping dragons in there, each the size of a large-ish newt.

'Let me go!' gasped Camicazi. 'They're only tiny dragons! They're quite sweet really...'

'Trust me,' said Hiccup grimly. *'Those are not sweet*. Those are Poisonous Piffleworms... For Thor's sake DO NOT WAKE THEM...'

Camicazi, Fishlegs, and Toothless froze in horror.

If a Piffleworm bites you, you have roughly one quarter of a second to curse your bad luck, before you fall to the ground as dead as a dodo.

How do you deal with a Poisonous Piffleworm?

12. A HERO'S GUIDE TO DEADLY DRAGONS

Hiccup had discovered how to deal with Poisonous Piffleworms some six months earlier, observing their behaviour one day dragon-watching at Wild Dragon Cliff. But in the terror of this moment, he couldn't quite remember what he had written in his notebook. He closed his eyes desperately... what was it now? He had a horrible feeling that you had to rub their tummies with the end of a nettle? No, on reflection, he thought that was Deadly Nadders... Thank goodness, because there weren't any nettles lying about... Did you blow in their eyes? No, that was Toxic Nightshades...

How do you deal with a Poisonous Piffleworm?

'What do we do now, Hiccup?' whispered Fishlegs, with his hands over his ears, trying to cut out the sound of those padding feet getting closer and closer.

'Do you think we can creep

139

through them without waking them up?'

As if in answer to this question, the nearest Piffleworm stirred in its sleep, opening its eyes briefly for a second, yawning and flicking out its little forked tongue, so that a droplet of purple venom landed on the edge of the brickwork.

It sizzled through the stone like acid, leaving a little puff of purple smoke rising from the hole.

The Piffleworm closed its eyes again.

'Oh, brother…' moaned Fishlegs.

If only Father hadn't confiscated my book… Hiccup thought to himself.

If only I had A Hero's Guide to Deadly Dragons *with me RIGHT NOW. Hang on a second… what am I thinking about? I do have* A Hero's Guide to Deadly Dragons *with me right now.*

Hiccup looked down at the big, heavy, dusty old book he was holding in his hand.

My ancestor must have written about Poisonous Piffleworms in here. Hiccup flung open the book.

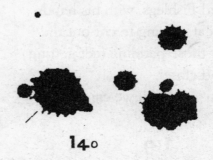

A Hero's Guide to Deadly Dragons

by Hiccup Horrendous Haddock III

There was a Warning on the first page,
written in large ink-smudged capitals.

WARNING!
READ *THE HERO'S*
GUIDE TO DEADLY DRAGONS
AND YOU WILL DIE

'We ALL die,' said Hiccup aloud,
'... eventually.'

WARNING

READ the
HERO'S GUIDE
TO DEADLY
DRAGONS
AND YOU
WILL DIE

… and this time he really did laugh.
For written on the next page were the words:

WE ALL DIE... EVENTUALLY.

Still laughing, he turned the next page...

… and disturbed a couple of real, live baby Piffleworms that had burrowed their way into the pages of the book and were steadily eating them. The Piffleworms froze for a second, and then the Piffleworm on the left gave a shriek of fury, and snapped forward its neck, pinpoint fangs bared to sink into Hiccup's hand and…

… Hiccup pulled his hand back in the nick of time, slammed the book shut, and threw it to the floor. Hastily, Fishlegs and Camicazi piled the heaviest books they could find on top of it.

'What do we do now?' whispered Fishlegs, his eyes round with terror.

The shriek of their fellow Pifbleworm had disturbed the sleep of the nest of Pifbleworms in the tunnel. They were squirming around restlessly, their eyelids flickering.

It was only a matter of minutes before they woke up.

'*How do you deal with a Pifleworm?*
How do you deal with a Pifleworm?' screeched Hiccup's brain. Was it that they couldn't stand the colour yellow? No, that was Deadly Nightshades... Was it that you tickled them behind the ears? No, that was Arsenic Adderwings. *What was it?*

Hiccup tried to imagine the page in his notebook in his mind's eye...

It seems a good moment, dear reader, to discover what kind of Hero YOU would make. Would you have lived through this situation? Being a Hero, and living to fight another day, is not just about swordfighting skills, you know. You also need a good memory, and an eye for detail.

Imagine, then, that the book you are holding RIGHT NOW contains a dragon so deadly that you cannot turn the pages back to find out How to Deal with a Pifleworm.

Now.

Don't cheat.

How do you deal with a Pifleworm?

How do you deal with a Pifleworm?

How do you deal with a Pifleworm? How? HOW? HOW?

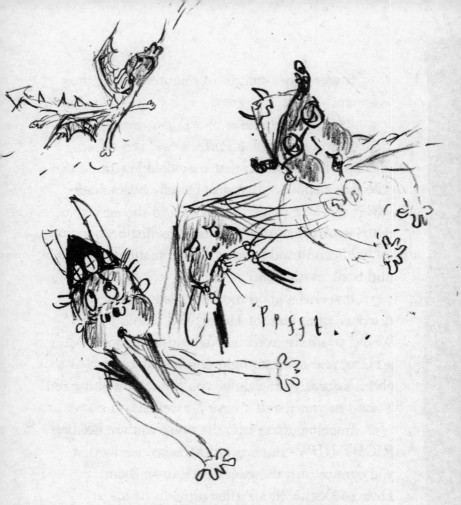

Pffft...

The answer is quite simple – or at least Hiccup
thought it was.

A Piffleworm cannot stand the sound of whistling.
The sound causes it to enter a frozen state of fear and
repulsion, where it cannot move a muscle or a whisker,

let alone a poison gland.

'Start whistling!' shrieked Hiccup. 'It makes them freeze and they can't hurt us then!'

'Are you sure?' screamed Fishlegs.

'No!' said Hiccup. 'I think it might be the thing with the nettle, but we haven't got any nettles here anyway!'

It is surprising how hard it is to whistle when you are frightened. All three of the Vikings, and Toothless too, did their best, but their throats were dry, and their lips were shaking, and the most whistle-y noise they could make was a sort of strangled puff.

Meanwhile the noise of approaching Driller-Dragons was so loud it was astonishing they weren't in the room already, and the Piffleworms were waking up, and were opening sleepy eyes, and the poison glands on their necks were beginning to swell up as they saw that their nest had been invaded by intruders...

'That's the worst whistling I've ever heard!' exclaimed Stormfly, circling above their heads in amusement.

'Stormfly!' cried Hiccup in relief. '*You* show us how to do it then!'

'Are you talking to me?' asked the Stormfly, pointing her wing at her chest.

'*Of course I'm talking to you!*' howled Hiccup.

'All right, all right, keep your hair on…' smiled the Stormfly, circling in graceful cartwheels around Hiccup's head, combing out her crest with one paw. 'You'll have to ask me nicely…'

'*PLEASE!*' shrieked all three Vikings simultaneously.

Stormfly puckered up her lips and stopped.

'But I can't remember anything to whistle,' she said slowly.

'Whistle ANYTHING!' screamed the Vikings.

Stormfly whistled the first verse of the Bog-Burglar National Anthem – not that she had a clue what it was, of course. By the end of the first couple of lines, the Piffleworms had frozen solid, puffed up like hard little dragon statues, with their mouths wide open and fangs bared.

Hiccup, Fishlegs, Camicazi and Toothless scrambled into the tunnel, trying to avoid stepping on the stone-like little monsters.

'Come on out now, Stormfly!' Hiccup ordered the Mood-dragon, who was still happily whistling as she flew upside down around the room.

'But the game isn't over!' Stormfly pointed out cheerily. 'They haven't found us yet!'

'*GET IN!*' shouted Hiccup, and he reached out and grabbed her by the tail, and dragged her into the tunnel.

But they were precious seconds too late.

With furious roars, four fully grown Driller-Dragons sprang like lions into the room.

Just a few moments later, and all they would have seen was an empty room. But the bookshelf-door was still wide open, and the three Vikings and two dragons were clearly to be seen, stuck in their hiding-place.

'*Now* they've found us!' squealed Stormfly in excitement. 'Coooeeeee!!!'

'Shut the door, Fishlegs!' screeched Camicazi and Hiccup, as the leading dragon leapt towards the three of them in the tunnel, and Fishlegs tried to shut the door…

… and the tip of the Driller-Dragon's drill caught in the crack between the door and the doorway, and Fishlegs could not shut it.

13. YIKES

The drill whirred furiously, and the three young Vikings were showered with splinters of wood as they all three hung on to the door.

The Driller-Dragon heaved back his mighty head and the door was ripped out of the Vikings' hands, and swung wide open again.

'Now, now!' sang the Stormfly. 'No rough stuff!'

The Driller-Dragon gave a roar of savage triumph and sprang forward, jaws agape.

And Hiccup picked a frozen Poisonous Piffleworm off the top of the tunnel, and threw it in the Driller-Dragon's face.

One second the dragon was this magnificent pouncing carnivore.

The next he was a mewling baby, gibbering with fear.

The Poisonous Piffleworm fell to the floor like a dragon made out of stone. But still, all four of the Driller-Dragons reared up on to their hind legs in horror, and turned around squealing, fighting to be the first to get out of the room.

Fishlegs slammed the bookshelf door.

They knelt on all fours, surrounded by an entire nest of unimaginably venomous frozen Piffleworms, the tunnel echoing with their pants of relief.

Hiccup shuffled on his knees to the end of the tunnel. They weren't as high up as they had been when the Stealth Dragon had dropped them off, but it was nonetheless a very long, long, way down, and Hiccup tried not to look.

He leaned out and called as loudly as he dared for the Stealth Dragon.

'Please, please let the Stealth Dragon hear us,' he prayed to Thor as he called.

Thor must have been listening – it has to be said, Thor has been very good to Hiccup over the years – for one second there was just bright blue sky in front of them, the next the sky had darkened slightly, in the ghostly form of the Secret Weapon.

'Ready to go, Sir?' asked the Stealth Dragon politely, hovering next to their tunnel.

'Well hello...' smirked the Stormfly, batting her eyelashes. 'Where did YOU spring from, gorgeous?'

Toothless swelled up with furious jealousy.

''Snot gorgeous! Is a g-g-great big invisible goody-goody!'

Fishlegs was delighted to make the dangerous crawl along the Stealth Dragon's outstretched hovering wing, so deeply relieved was he to get out of that Library.

'Where to, Sir?' asked the Stealth Dragon, when all three of them had fastened their seatbelts.

'Next stop the ISLE OF BERK,' said Hiccup.

The Stealth Dragon wheeled around on his albatross wings, and for the first time Hiccup realised that there was a most unpleasant smell of rotten eggs in the air, and they were not alone in the Archipelago skies.

The air was full of dragons, dragons as far as the eye could see.

An entire Dragon Army was descending on the little Isle of Forget Me.

These were large riding-dragons, but in this case, because this was an attack operation, they weren't being RIDDEN exactly.

Each dragon had a heavily armed Viking Warrior dangling from his claws. The Warriors had their swords drawn, and they were screaming the Murderous War Cry at the tops of their lungs. The Murderous Tribe was storming the Meathead Public Library.

It was rather beautiful to watch the precision

of their attack.

The dragons swooped down to the Library
Entrance, and let the Warriors go at exactly the right
moment so that they could hit the ground running, and
could launch immediately into fighting the Meatheads,
who poured out to greet them.

A pitched battle was taking place, and the
Murderous Tribe were winning, because they are some
of the best barbarians in the business.

'HA!' whispered Fishlegs to Camicazi. 'So much
for this Stealth Dragon being un-trackable! Five
minutes later and Madguts would have caught us
red-handed!'

'MMMmmm, you could be right,' admitted

Camicazi guiltily. 'We'd better tell my mother she needs to get rid of it as soon as possible.'

Hiccup got the Stealth Dragon to fly on a lower flight path than normal back to Berk. And it seemed as if the entire way, above them was this steady stream of Murderous Dragons flying in the other direction.

'That disgusting smell,' mused Stormfly, wrinkling her beautiful nostrils and peering upwards as she flew, 'it really reminds me of something and I can't think what…'

There is a narrow gap

called the Slice of Death that separates the North Meathead Island from the South Meathead Island. Most Vikings tend to avoid it, because there are shoals of dangerous reefs all the way along.

But Camicazi steered straight towards it, and once they had entered the canyon, the Stealth Dragon didn't bother to fly any higher above the waves. He just swerved to avoid the rocks as if he were doing a slalom in the air.

The impossibly high walls of the Cliff of Forever soared up to their left.

The improbably high walls of the Cliff of Eternity stretched up to their right.

And the Stealth Dragon swivelled his way through the rocks at the bottom of this tunnel of cliff like he was threading a needle through the treacherous surf. By the time they shot out of the Slice of Death, all three Vikings and their dragons were drenched with spray.

Even Fishlegs forgot about the disgusting smell sufficiently to join the others in whooping with excitement as they were soaked by another wave, drenched in salt, and ears blown backward in the wind.

He might not have felt so happy if he could have seen the sinister dark figure standing in front of the Meathead Public Library, fingering his axes. It was

Madguts the Murderous, on the path of his stolen Stealth Dragon, his tracker-dragons sniffing through the sand in a frenzy of excitement.

'He's been here...' hissed Gumboil. 'But he's already left flying thataway...' And he pointed a black-gloved finger in the direction of the little Isle of Berk.

This way to the Isle of Berk...

14. MADGUTS WILL BE STEAMING MAD

Stoick had a difficult afternoon of not finding things. Firstly he was looking for the *How to Train Your Dragon* book. Then he couldn't find his son, because he felt that maybe he had been a little crosser than he should have been, particularly given that it was Hiccup's birthday.

But both book and son had vanished into thin air, even though he had sent half the Tribe all over Berk looking for them. As the sun began to sink that evening, Big-Boobied Bertha stomped into his Chiefly Hut, with a confident smirk on her face.

The mighty bosoms of Big-Boobied Bertha had killed many a Warrior in mortal combat. She was a great monster of a woman, who closely resembled a Woolly Mammoth in a dress, and even in a one-on-one social situation she tended to bellow at the top of her fog-horn voice, as if she was trying to be heard by troops at the other end of a large-ish battlefield.

'So *this* is where you're hiding, is it, Stoick, you old Warthog?' she yelled cheerfully, giving him a playful tug on the whiskers that made him bristle furiously.

'Hoping you can skulk in here till I'll forget about the bet, are you? Well, I haven't. It's the end of the day, your time's up, and I hope you're ready to give me those axes. Where's your proof that you lettuce-hearted, rabbit-brained, butter-fingered Hooligans are better at burglary than us Bog-Burglars?'

Stoick's chest swelled with indignation. 'We Hooligans are the finest Burglars in the *world*!' he yelled, punching his fist in the air. 'One of my Warriors, Gobber the Belch, has stolen a book from the Meathead Public Library, from right under the nose of the Hairy Scary Librarian! An act of Burglary and Bravery of the highest order!'

'Not bad, not bad,' whistled Bertha. 'I wouldn't have thought that that great lumbering sack of potatoes had it in him.' She looked cheerfully round the room. 'So, where is it then?'

'What?' asked Stoick, playing for time.

'The book, man, the book! The book that your Gobber-with-the-face-like-a-hippopotamus-that-somebody-trod-on has fluke-ily snaffled from that loon the Librarian. Where is it?'

Stoick's chest deflated a little. 'Ah, yes, well, that's what I can't quite understand. I had the book in this very room only this morning, but now it seems to have completely disappeared. It's most extraordinary. I'm afraid you're going to have to take my word for it...'

Big-Boobied Bertha hadn't heard such a good joke in ages. She laughed so hard the tears ran down her beard and she could barely stand up. 'HA! HA! HA! HA!' roared Big-Boobied Bertha. 'Oh that's a good one! You stole the book and then you seem to have *lost* it, is that what you're saying?' jeered Bertha. 'Fiddlesticks and tadpole tails! You never HAD this book you're boasting about because you hopeless Hooligans couldn't burgle berries from a baby!'

Stoick wondered whether to hit her.

'Never mind, Stoick,' boomed Bertha, giving him a friendly dig in the ribs, 'even if you HAD stolen that silly little book of yours, you wouldn't have won the bet anyway. Come and see what *I* stole from Madguts the Murderous only yesterday... Follow me...'

Muttering rude words under his breath to the great god Thor, Stoick followed Bertha's bossy departing bottom all the way to the Dragon Stables.

Bertha stopped outside a particularly large stable door, and began to undo the bolts. 'I hope you don't mind that I borrowed an empty stable of yours to put it in... this will show you what a REAL burglar can do...'

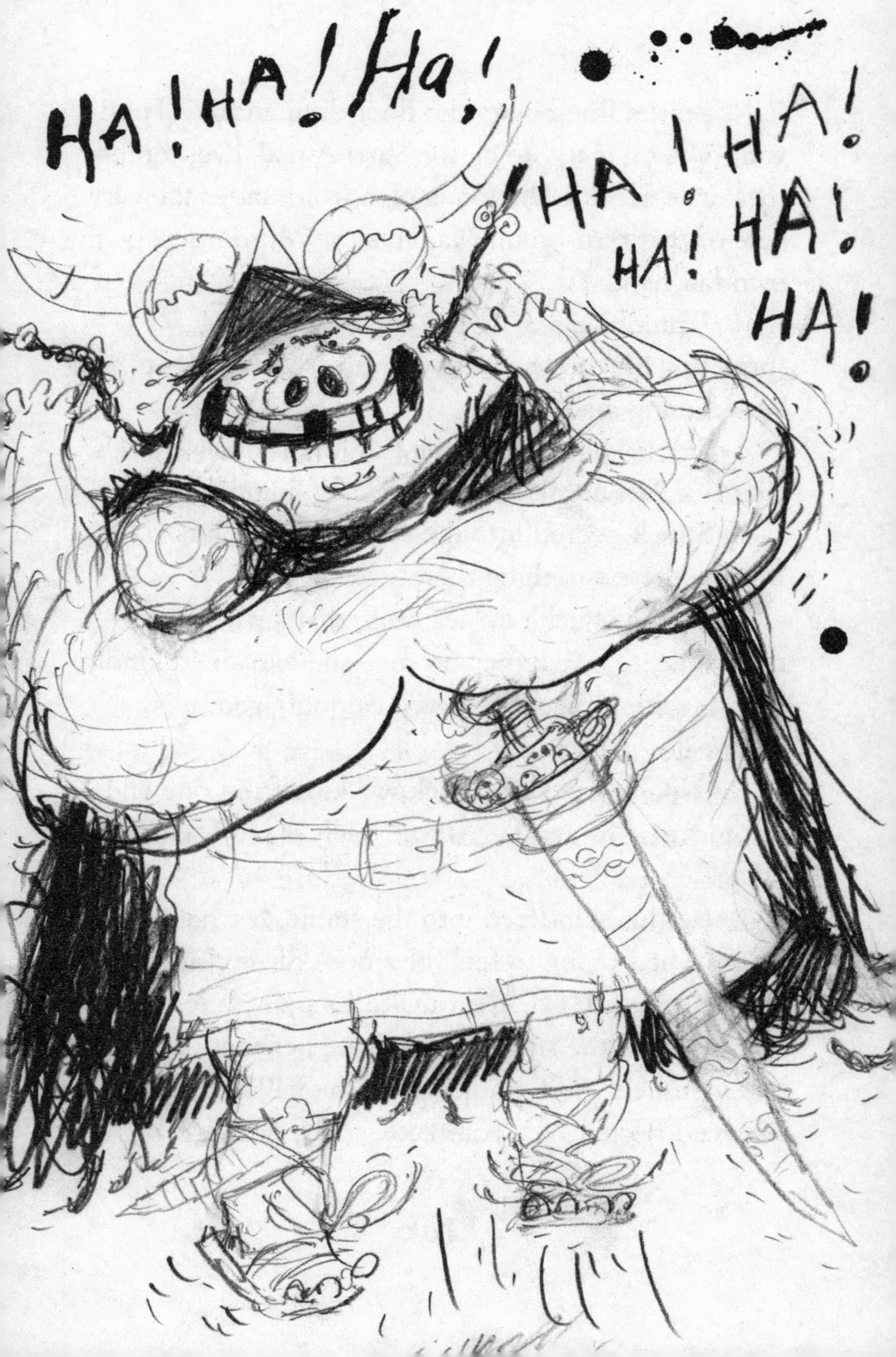
HA! HA! Ha,
HA! HA! HA! HA! HA! HA!

Bertha flung open the door dramatically. 'Feast your eyes on *that*, Stoick the Vast! A real, live, top-of-the-range Stealth Dragon, stolen from under the very *nose* of that bird-brain, Madguts the Murderous, by my own fair hands!'

'Thumbnails of Thor!' exclaimed Stoick, forgetting his fury, he was so impressed. 'Madguts will be steaming mad!'

'Pooh!' boasted Bertha proudly, if unwisely. 'Us Bog-Burglars aren't scared of THAT idiotic stinkpot!'

Stoick peered into the stable. 'But... but... but Bertha, there's nothing there...'

Bertha chuckled. 'Yes, well, that's what makes them a Secret Weapon, you see,' she explained kindly. 'The Stealth Dragon is so well camouflaged, it is practically invisible...'

'No, *really*,' said Stoick, walking from one end of the stable to another, 'there really *is* NOTHING HERE.'

Bertha blundered into the stable, her hands in front of her, trying to feel for a not-only-invisible-but-absolutely-NOT-THERE Stealth Dragon. It took three turns around the stable to convince her that the dragon had vanished. 'Well bother my bunions!' exclaimed Big-Boobied Bertha. 'It's completely disappeared!'

Stoick began to laugh.

'It was here this morning! Large as life and as transparent as glass!' protested Bertha.

'Oh, yes,' jeered Stoick, laughing like a drain, 'invisible dragons, my belly-button! That's a good one, Bertha, that's a good one! I'll give you a couple of *invisible* axes in return for winning the bet!'

Big-Boobied Bertha turned purple as a blueberry and clenched her fists. The two of them were so engrossed in their disagreement that they did not notice a tall, thin figure creeping up behind them.

'Both of you hold your hands above your heads and come slowly out of the stable!' barked a hissing croak of a voice.

15. THE HAIRY LIBRARIAN GETS SCARY

Bertha jumped a foot in the air and her plaits shot out from the side of her head, all of a tremble. She spun around with really quite impressive quickness for a woman of her girth, and nearly fainted with relief when she saw it was only the Hairy Scary Librarian, standing in the stable doorway with a Northbow pulled back ready to shoot.

'Oooh, Hairy, it's only you, thank Thor,' she said, pressing her hand to her gigantic chest. 'I thought you might be Madguts the Murderous...'

'SHUT IT, BERTHA, AND PUT YOUR THIEVING HANDS OVER YOUR BURGLAROUS HEAD,' advised the Librarian.

It occurred to Bertha and Stoick that the Librarian was looking rather more agitated than normal. He had always been a little unstable, but the Itchyworms-down-the-trousers-incident had driven him over the edge. There was a mad glint in his eye, a large lump on his head, and a stray Itchyworm left down one side was making his whole body tremble.

'Err... you're looking a little peaky, Hairy,' said

Bertha, politely humouring the Librarian by putting her hands over her head. 'Do you think you need a little lie-down?'

'YOU BETCHA I'M LOOKING A LITTLE BIT PEAKY!' shrieked the Hairy Scary Librarian. 'YOUR LITTLE HOOLIGAN AND BOG-BURGLAR BRATS HAS BEEN SNEAKINGS INTO MY LIBRARY, AND STEALING ONE OF MY BOOKS!'

'I DON'T KNOW WHAT YOU'RE TALKING ABOUT!' roared Stoick the Vast, genuinely bewildered. 'AND HOW DARE YOU THREATEN *ME*, STOICK THE VAST, ON MY VERY OWN ISLAND! GET OFF MY LAND, OR I WILL THROW YOU OFF!'

'*You* are on the wrong end of this arrow,' pointed out the Hairy Scary Librarian, 'and therefore not in a position to give out orders. Your brats have been trespassing,' he continued, 'and have stolen one of my books...'

'You must have mistaken them for somebody else,' said Stoick the Vast, with less of a bellow as he realised that the Hairy Scary Librarian had a point about the being-on-the-wrong-end-of-the-arrow. 'One barbarian child looks very like another...'

'Not *your* child,' screeched the Librarian, '*your* child is very different from most decent Viking children... small skinny boy with bright red hair, ridiculously scrawny for the son of a Chief...'

'There are *lots* of Viking children who haven't had their growth spurt yet!' protested Stoick defiantly. 'It could have been *anybody*!'

'Was with a boy with a face like a fish and a girl with light fingers and no manners,' continued the Hairy Scary Librarian.

'My Camicazi isn't the nicking-things *type*!' cried Big-Boobied Bertha.

(Bertha had

her fingers firmly crossed above her head.)

'*All* Bog-Burglars is the nicking-things *type!*' screeched the Hairy Scary Librarian. 'They'd nick the trees from the woods if they could fit 'em in they's pockets! And I caughts the little magpies *red-handed* pilfering my very last copy of *How to Train Your Dragon!*' screeched the Librarian.

Stoick started guiltily.

'HA!' cried the Librarian triumphantly. 'So you *do* knows what I is talking about! You all try and steal books off me, don't you, and fair enough I suppose, we are Vikings, but those who gets caught in my Library have to pay the price, which is death on the spot, no questions asked. But *did* they's have the decency to put their hands up and let me poke them with my Heart-Slicers?' His hissing, whiny voice rose in outrage. 'Oh no, not them, they bonked me on the head, and put Itchyworms down my trousers! I don't know what the younger generation is coming to!'

Stoick the Vast couldn't help grinning with pride when he heard this information. *Well done, Hiccup!* he thought exultantly.

Stoick's secret smile drove the Hairy Scary Librarian wild with temper, and he let fly the arrow, which cut off Big-Boobied Bertha's left plait, and he had fastened another arrow in the bow before Bertha and Stoick had had time to blink.

'TELL ME WHERE THE THIEVING LITTLE MAGPIES IS OR THE NEXT ARROW GOES INTO STOICK HERE.'

Bertha tried to bluster her way out of the situation. 'I really don't know what you're talking about,' she bellowed, 'and I haven't seen my daughter since this morning anyway.'

The Hairy Scary Librarian let fly his next arrow, which flew straight into the chest of Stoick the Vast.

And this was where the Hairy Scary Librarian lost control of the situation.

For instead of falling down as dead as a dinosaur, Stoick calmly removed the arrow from his breast and snapped it in two.

'B-b-but that's impossible!' stammered the Hairy Scary Librarian, turning very white. 'HOW IS YOU DOING THAT?'

The Northbow is the deadliest, hardest, most accurate bow in the Archipelago. *Nobody* gets hit by a Northbow arrow and lives to tell the tale.

The Hairy Scary Librarian re-loaded his bow and was about to shoot again.

But he didn't get the chance.

An enormous, practically invisible dragon appeared out of nowhere and landed on him.

Squashing him.

Flat.

16. THE LIBRARIAN GETS SQUASHED

Hiccup, Camicazi, and Fishlegs were hoping to secretly replace the *How to Train Your Dragon* book without anyone finding out that it had ever been burnt, and return the Stealth Dragon before it was discovered that they had stolen it.

However, leaning over the edge of the Stealth Dragon's invisible wings, Hiccup could see the two corpulent figures of his father and Camicazi's mother, standing in front of the open stable door, and the thin furious form of the Hairy Scary Librarian with his loaded bow.

The plan changed in an instant. 'Land on that skinny Viking with the stupidly long beard, Stealth Dragon!' shrieked Hiccup, 'as quick and as hard as you can!' And the Secret Weapon obligingly went into a shrieking dive that had Fishlegs covering his eyes, and the Stormfly whooping with excitement, and Toothless complaining that he was 'showing off a-a-again.'

The mighty shining form of the Stealth Dragon landed with considerable force and pin-point accuracy right on top of the elderly madman.

17. THE NUMBER SIX SWORD

For once in their lives Stoick the Vast and Big-Boobied Bertha were completely and entirely lost for words.

Stoick the Vast's mighty jaw dropped in his amazement. 'By the Black Heart and Tricky Twisting Tongue of the Great God Loki!' he cried, for he had never seen a Stealth Dragon before, and his first thought was, that perhaps Thor had decided to save their lives by taking out his hammer and knocking a piece out of the sky to strike down the enraged Librarian.

Even Big-Boobied Bertha's tremendous breasts heaved in their astonishment.

And they only heaved the more at the sight of three little figures climbing carefully down from the back of the great shimmering mirage of Madguts's Secret Weapon.

'Ooooh, well done, you great magnificent hunk of a dragon!' cooed the Stormfly, fluttering around the Stealth Dragon's mighty head, batting her eyelashes. 'Brilliantly flattened!'

'Is not so b-b-brilliant just to s-s-squash

Toothless can do s-s-squashing! Look!

boing boing boing

somebody!' hissed Toothless, in a jealous fury. '*Anyone* can do s-s-squashing! Look! Toothless can do squashing too!'

And the little dragon jumped up and down on the end of one of the Hairy Scary Librarian's long, quivering feet, poking out from beneath the beautiful gleaming bottom of the Stealth Dragon.

'Camicazi!' scolded Big-Boobied Bertha furiously. 'I might have known it! What HAVE you been doing with MY stolen goods!'

Camicazi was clearly no more afraid of her mother than she was of anyone else.

She put her hands on her hips. 'Well I like

THAT!' she exclaimed. 'We SWOOP down, saving your neck in the nick of time from being shot by this mad Librarian guy and all you can do is COMPLAIN!'

'AND WHY,' thundered Big-Boobied Bertha, in a fog-horn voice so loud that it made the ear-drums of the listening Vikings vibrate, 'IS THIS LIBRARIAN SHOOTING AT US IN THE FIRST PLACE? I TOLD YOU THE LAST TIME I RESCUED YOU FROM THE DUNGEONS OF THE DANGER-BRUTES, THERE ARE CERTAIN PEOPLE YOU NICK FROM, LIKE THE PEACEABLES, AND THE QUIET-LIFES, AND CERTAIN PEOPLE THAT YOU DON'T BECAUSE IT'S JUST TOO DANGEROUS, I MEAN, HOW MANY TIMES DO I HAVE TO SAY THIS, CAMICAZI.'

Like many parents, Big-Boobied Bertha was making an EXCELLENT point that she would have done well to have listened to *herself*, for she was so busy scolding, and everybody else was so busy listening, that nobody had noticed a sinister, thuggish figure landing his dragon a hundred yards away, and nobody had seen him quietly drawing out his axes, a horrible grin on his ugly mug, and a truly unpleasant reeking smell of rotting eggs and stinking haddock pouring out from between his jagged and broken teeth.

Nobody, that is, apart from the Stormfly, who suddenly stopped mid-flutter, and wrinkled up her pretty little nose. 'Ooooh, *yuck*!' she exclaimed disgustedly. 'What *is* that revolting SMELL?'

Smell is one of the strongest of our senses, and the powerful pong given off by the Murderous Tribe at close quarters reactivated the part of Stormfly's brain that had been shut off by the blow to the head in the Library, and her memory returned.

'Why, I do believe it's that human stink-bomb Madguts the Murderous!' she cried in delight. 'It's all coming back to me now! I am the Stormfly, and I spent my earliest dragonhood in their whiffy Murderous Mountains.'

Stoick the Vast, Big-Boobied Bertha, Hiccup, Camicazi and Fishlegs turned very pale, and slowly round, and there he was, the revolting smell himself, Madguts the Murderous, his cold staring blue eyes like chips of ice.

Madguts was not alone. He was accompanied, at a respectful distance behind, by about fifty or so crack Stealth Warriors, who had been dropped by their dragons on silent wings, and were now all training their Northbows straight at the chest of Big-Boobied Bertha.

Madguts grunted something inarticulate to his

henchman Gumboil. 'The Number Six Sword, Your
Viciousness?' replied Gumboil to his Master, removing
the bag of weaponry from his back and searching
through it. 'A very fine choice, if I may say so, Sir.
Extra-Long, Super-Deadly. The Number Six will never
fail you in a Revenge Situation.'

Gumboil removed a truly evil-looking sword from
the basket, and handed it to Madguts, who tested the
point of it on his hand for sharpness, sending a bright
sprinkle of blood down on to the ground.

Bertha swallowed hard.

18. WHY NO ONE STEALS FROM MADGUTS

Madguts gestured towards his henchman, Gumboil, who always did his talking for him.

'Madguts is interested to hear, Bertha,' sneered Gumboil, while everybody gave a horrified gasp and tried not to breathe in too deeply, 'that you feel there are some people it would be unwise to nick things from. Because he would have thought that *he* would be one of those people.'

'Oh, you are, Madguts,

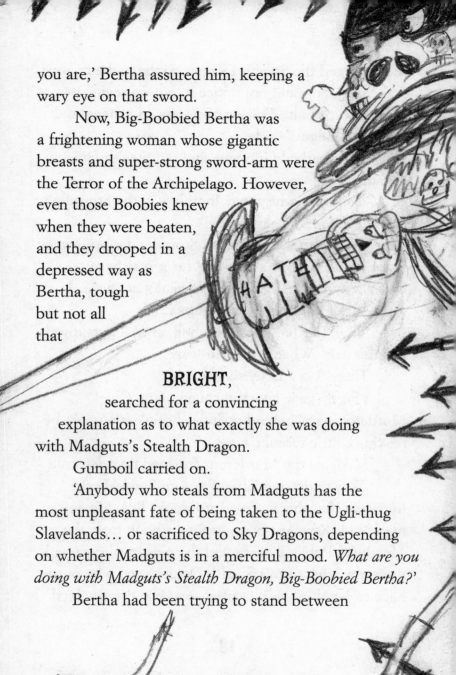

you are,' Bertha assured him, keeping a wary eye on that sword.

Now, Big-Boobied Bertha was a frightening woman whose gigantic breasts and super-strong sword-arm were the Terror of the Archipelago. However, even those Boobies knew when they were beaten, and they drooped in a depressed way as Bertha, tough but not all that

BRIGHT,

searched for a convincing explanation as to what exactly she was doing with Madguts's Stealth Dragon.

Gumboil carried on.

'Anybody who steals from Madguts has the most unpleasant fate of being taken to the Ugli-thug Slavelands… or sacrificed to Sky Dragons, depending on whether Madguts is in a merciful mood. *What are you doing with Madguts's Stealth Dragon, Big-Boobied Bertha?*'

Bertha had been trying to stand between

Madguts and the Stealth Dragon, in the pathetic hope that Madguts would not notice it, but on seeing its Master, the Stealth Dragon had leapt to its feet, and slunk to Madguts's side.

'SIT!' barked Gumboil, and the Stealth Dragon instantly sat.

'You see?' whispered Toothless in the Stormfly's ear. 'He's a real goody-goody!'

'He is, isn't he?' replied Stormfly disapprovingly. She sighed. 'And he's working for a real baddy-baddy... a very STINKY baddy-baddy at that... I can't think WHAT I saw in him...'

'Well, Bertha?' said Gumboil, as Madguts toyed with his axe. 'What is your answer?'

There was a nasty silence.

Hiccup gave a tactful cough. 'Um, Chief Murderous, sir,' he said politely, 'I think you might be making a little mistake here...'

Madguts the Murderous frowned thunderously.

'Very understandable, I'm sure,' said Hiccup, hurriedly, 'but this is not what it looks like. Me and my friends have just been stealing a book from the Meathead Public Library, and the person who chased us on the back of this Stealth Dragon, and who must have stolen it in the first place, was not Big-Boobied

Bertha but the *Hairy Scary Librarian...*'

Hiccup pointed to the prone and squashed figure of the Hairy Scary Librarian. He was still alive, but gently slumbering in the heather. '... Big-Boobied Bertha was in the middle of arresting him when you arrived.'

'Brilliant...' whispered Camicazi under her breath. 'That's *brilliant*... for a boy of course...'

The Hairy Scary Librarian would have hotly denied this charge, but the Hairy Scary Librarian was in no condition to deny *anything*, as he slumbered peacefully on, out for the count.

'In fact,' continued Hiccup, 'you should really be *thanking* Big-Boobied Bertha here, because the moment she clapped eyes on the creature, she knew that such a splendid Secret Weapon could only belong to a magnificent Murderous Chieftain such as yourself, sir – which is why she squashed him. Isn't that right, Bertha?'

'Oh, ah... *yes*,' said Big-Boobied Bertha hurriedly, 'that's absolutely right.'

Everybody held their breaths as Madguts the Murderous looked from Hiccup to Big-Boobied Bertha to the slumbering Librarian, from out of his mean blue eyes, as cold and cruel as the ocean itself.

He chewed thoughtfully on his knuckle-bone
for a moment or two, and then he advanced towards
Bertha with his terrifying sword gleaming in his hand.
Bertha raised her head bravely, for a Bog-Burglar
laughs in the face of death, and looked Madguts
straight in the eye as she waited for the final blow…

… And to her astonishment, Madguts GAVE her
the sword.

And then Madguts leaned over, spat in the
heather, and motioned to his henchman. He grunted
something in the Gumboil's ear, and then, without a
word, he climbed up on to the Stealth Dragon's back,

to Bertha's
astonishment,
he GAVE her
the sword…

and the beautiful creature sprang into the air, turning in an instant from as green as the heather to as blue as the sky, and was gone.

'Madguts gives you his sword in thanks for your services in capturing the fool who tried to steal his Stealth Dragon,' sneered Gumboil. '*He* seems to believe your story... *I* don't, mind you, but Madguts is the boss. GUARDS!' screamed the Gumboil, removing the Heart-Slicers from the Librarian's sword-belt, and adding them to his own. 'TAKE THIS DOZY LIBRARIAN OFF TO THE UGLI-THUG SLAVELANDS!'

The Guards snapped to attention, and one of their dragons took the limp body of the unconscious Librarian in-between its claws and flew off with it towards the west.

The Hairy Scary Librarian would wake up many hours later, deep in the heart of the Ugli-thug Slavelands, rather thinner than he was before, and with a thumping headache, and his temper would not be improved once he realised where he was.

Lest there are any soft-hearted readers out there, who are worrying about his unjust fate, I should remind you that he was a singularly unpleasant character who had dispatched many an unfortunate

Warrior up to Valhalla with his Heart-Slicers, for no greater crime than attempting to burgle a book from the Library in order to impress their fellow Tribesmen. So I wouldn't feel too sorry for him if I was you.

The Gumboil spat on the ground in as disgusting a way as his Master. *He* didn't seem too sorry for the Librarian. 'Serve him right for falling asleep,' he said, with a sneering grin like a malevolent toad. 'And fortunate for him that Madguts was in a merciful mood. I'll be looking out for you, Bertha...' he warned the Big-Boobied one, 'I wouldn't do any more burgling from the Murderous Tribe... the next time you do it you may not be so lucky...'

And with that, the Murderous Warriors climbed up on to the backs of their riding-dragons, leaving behind them a faint, sulphurous whiff of haddock and bad eggs.

19. HICCUP'S BIRTHDAY PRESENT

Bertha waited until they were safely out of earshot, and then she shook her fist up at the sky and shouted, 'THAT'S RIGHT, OFF YOU GO, YOU IDIOTIC OLD STINK-POT, US BOG-BURGLARS AREN'T AFRAID OF *YOU*, YOU KNOW!'

'Well,' sighed Big-Boobied Bertha, '*that* was a close one! I have got to admit, Stoick, that skinny prawn of a son of yours may not look up to much, and he may not be able to burgle for toffee, but he can certainly think on his feet.'

'He sure as Thor *can* burgle for toffee!' objected Stoick, thumping his son delightedly on the back. 'He's burgled a book from the Meathead Public Library – where is the book, Hiccup?'

Silently, Hiccup reached inside his backpack and drew out the *How to Train Your Dragon* book – second edition, and handed it to Stoick.

'Not to mention stealing a Secret Weapon from you and Madguts the Murderous. Not bad for a twelve-year-old, I'd say. And, what's more, he's PROVED that Hooligans are JUST as good at

Burglary as Bog-Burglars. So I think you'll find that *I've* won our little bet... You'd better stump up those axes, Bertha, like a good little loser...'

Stoick rubbed his hands together in glee.

Of course, Big-Boobied Bertha could NEVER be described as a 'good little loser', and she swelled up in fury, her beard bristling and her ham-like fists a-clench. But she was a good sport at heart, and a Viking of her word. And after all, young Hiccup here *had* just saved her from an unpleasant spell in the Ugli-thug Slavelands... She'd have *escaped* of course, for you can't keep a Bog-Burglar under lock and key, but it would have been a nasty experience nonetheless...

So her stormy brow cleared, and she reached into her axe-belt and brought out two of her finest axes, and gave them to Stoick with reasonable good humour.

After all, at the end of the day, she had lost two axes but gained a rather magnificent sword, and a Murderous sword is hard to come by.

'EXCELLENT!' roared Stoick the Vast. 'I hope you'll join us this evening for Hiccup's Birthday Banquet?'

'BUT OF COURSE!' thundered Big-Boobied Bertha, rubbing her hands together excitedly, for she was always the life and soul of the party.

'I shall be presenting him with a new sword as a birthday present!' boomed Stoick, trying (unsuccessfully), to sound careless and not BURSTING with pride at his son's achievements this afternoon. 'A sword suitable for a boy who is now a twelve-year-old and the son of a Viking Chief... not to mention a Burglar of some distinction...'

'Um, Father,' interrupted Hiccup. 'I'm quite pleased with my *old* sword really... there's something ELSE that I would really like as a birthday present...'

'You can have ANYTHING!' promised Stoick, rashly, because he was so delighted to have won his bet against Big-Boobied Bertha. 'Anything at all! Axes, spears, a new dragon, anything at all!'

'Well...' said Hiccup slowly, 'what I would really really like now the Hairy Scary Librarian is got rid of, is for books not to be banned, and that Library to be open to the public again. Those Driller-Dragons are making an awful mess of the place.'

Stoick's brows descended angrily. This wasn't what he had been thinking of at all!

'I KNOW you think *How to Train Your Dragon* is the only book worth having, and that Vikings don't need books, but there are LOADS of books in that Library that you would find incredibly useful,' pleaded

Hiccup, 'books about swordfighting, about axe-work, about all the different types of dragons. Books with maps in, that will help you sail to Africa, and India and America…'

'No such place!' snorted Stoick.

'We nearly DIED in that Library,' said Hiccup, 'but we didn't because we knew How to Deal with a Piffleworm. And that's how books can help you, Father. They can save your life, they really can…'

Stoick looked thoughtful. From out of his breast pocket he drew the scruffy copy of *A Hero's Guide to Deadly Dragons* that he had confiscated from Hiccup earlier that morning.

This notebook really HAD saved Stoick's life, only ten minutes earlier.

For when the Hairy Scary Librarian shot that arrow, the sharp point of it had sunk into the *book* rather than into Stoick's chest. It had nearly cut the poor bedraggled book in half, so deep had been the wound.

Maybe it was a sign from Thor.

Perhaps books weren't as dangerous as they looked, and maybe they really *could* be useful to the Viking Tribes. He'd always wanted to go to Africa...

'MMMmmm,' grunted Stoick the Vast. He handed *A Hero's Guide to Deadly Dragons* back to Hiccup.

A Viking Chief SHOULDN'T change his mind... thought Stoick. So he tried to sound as stern and Chiefly as he could, in the hope that nobody would notice. 'Um, I REALLY think you need to write this book out again, Hiccup,' scolded Stoick sternly. 'Look at it, it's in a disgraceful state. And as for that other matter... I'll speak to "the Thing" about it.'

Hiccup grinned delightedly.

Stoick the Vast and Big-Boobied Bertha stomped

Stoick gives Hiccup his birthday present.

off, spiritedly discussing Axe-Fighting Moves, and who was the better Wrestler.

...But OF COURSE I'm a better axe-fighter than you are, Stoick, you Hooligans couldn't fight your way out of a paper bag, why I bet you two of my finest swords that...

'Happy birthday, Hiccup,' smiled Fishlegs.
'You must admit,' said Camicazi, looking at Hiccup a trifle anxiously, 'it's been a really good one.'

Hiccup clasped *A Hero's Guide to Deadly Dragons* to his chest.

When you only have a birthday once every four years, it IS important that it's a good one.

He surveyed the day. On the whole, it wasn't *quite* what he'd *hoped* for, which was a really quiet, peaceful twenty-four hours.

He'd stolen a Secret Weapon belonging to Madguts the Murderous. He'd knocked out a Driller-Dragon. He'd narrowly avoided being stuck on the end of one of the Hairy Scary Librarian's Heart-Slicers. He'd been lost in a Labyrinth. He'd discovered the Dragon-whisperer's Way. He'd dealt with an entire nest of Piffleworms. He rescued his father from death by Northbow, and Big-Boobied Bertha from being sent to the Ugli-thug Slavelands...

Just a normal day in the Barbaric Archipelago, really.

But it had all turned out all right in the end.

Thor only knows how...

And this was the surprising thing about life on Berk. It was a bit like the sea itself. One minute it was all storms, and shipwrecks, and desperate escapes from deadly dragons, the next it was as calm, and peacefully restful, as if these things had never happened.

The sun had gone down now, and the stars were beginning to come out in a darkening sky, reflected like candles in the glass-flat Bay below. Further down the hillside, in the Hooligan Village, fires were being lit in preparation for the Birthday Banquet, and the first sounds of singing could be heard.

Rather surprisingly, despite being some of the roughest, toughest rabble of plug-ugly Barbarians you could ever have the misfortune to come across, the Hooligans were *excellent* singers, and their deep, gorgeous voices rose up with the plumes of smoke, in gentle, peaceful harmony.

Hiccup gave a sigh of contentment.

Hiccup was extremely fond of his family, but he didn't always find it easy being so very very different from the rest of his Hooligan relations.

If Toothless and Camicazi hadn't drawn him into the Library Labyrinth, he would never have discovered that he had a *secret ancestor*, someone with the same name and the same interests as Hiccup himself.

And somehow this discovery made him feel a lot

less lonely in the world…

'Yup,' said Hiccup. 'What with one thing and another, it's been an EXCELLENT birthday.'

Camicazi turned a celebratory cartwheel.

Hiccup began to stroll down to the Banquet with his good friends Fishlegs and Camicazi, their way down to the Village lit up by the little sparks of

flickering Glow-worms, shining deep in the darkness of the bracken.

'Are you coming to the B-b-banquet, Stormfly?' asked a blushing Toothless from his perch on Hiccup's helmet.

'I might,' replied the Stormfly carelessly, swooping down low over a marsh they were passing, in order to admire her reflection in the water. 'Nobody knows what the Stormfly might do...'

'*Toothless* knows where they k-k-keeping the food...' suggested Toothless eagerly.

At the mention of food, Stormfly's yellow eyes lit up. 'Lead on, O Gummy One,' drawled the Stormfly.

The two little dragons flew off in the direction of the Village, and Hiccup called out anxiously after them, 'You're NOT to go nicking the food now, Toothless, before the Banquet's even begun! Remember, YOU got us into all this trouble *in the first place*... be good, now, Toothless!'

Stormfly batted her beautiful long eyelashes. 'Oh, we wouldn't dream of stealing any food, or causing any trouble, would we, Toothless?' she called out over her shoulder. 'Don't you worry, Anxious-Human-with-Freckles, Stormfly will keep an eye on him, you can trust the Stormfly...'

And as the two little dragons soared downward towards the quiet and restful unsuspecting Village

below, even in the darkness of the evening Hiccup
could see the elegant swooping little form of
the Mood-dragon blush from gold, to violet,
to deepest indigo, as she flew.

But how can we know that dragons did not exist? We have never actually BEEN to the Dark Ages.

EPILOGUE BY HICCUP HORRENDOUS HADDOCK THE THIRD, THE LAST OF THE GREAT VIKING HEROES.

So that is the story of how, on my twelfth birthday, I came to liberate the Meathead Public Library.

My father kept his promise, and gave a passionate speech at the next meeting of 'The Thing' arguing that books were not dangerous, but could be helpful to the Viking Tribes. And such was his influence at that meeting, that the ban on books was lifted, the Library was open to the public once more, and the Driller-Dragons were prevented from grazing in its halls.

I have spent many happy hours in that very Library, wandering down the quiet corridors, and opening each book is like opening a door into other times, other worlds. It reminds of me of that time when I discovered the Dragon-whisperer's Way...

I myself grew up to be not only a Hero, but also a Writer. When I was an adult, I re-wrote *A Hero's Guide to Deadly Dragons*, and I included not only some descriptions of the various deadly dragon species, and a useful Dragonese Dictionary, but also this story of how the book came to be written in the first place.

This is the book that you are holding in your hands right now.

Perhaps you even borrowed it from a Library?

If so, thank Thor that the sinister figure of the Hairy Scary Librarian is not lurking round a corner, hiding in the shadows, Heart-Slicers at the ready, or that the punishment for your curiosity is not the whirring whine of a Driller-Dragon's drill.

You, dear reader, I am sure cannot *imagine* what it might be like to live in a world in which books are banned.

For surely, such things will never happen in the Future?

Thank Thor that you live in a time and a place

And spare
a thought
for those

where people have the right to live and think and write and read their books in peace, and there are no need for Heroes any more…

And spare a thought for those who have not been so lucky.

ho have not been so LUCKY.

DRAGON PROFILES

stinkdragons

~ STATISTICS ~

COLOURS: A very gaudy orange, with big black stripes

ARMED WITH: A smell so disgusting it makes you fall over.

FEAR FACTOR: Nobody is **TERRIFIED** of Stinkdragons, because they can't actually **KILL** you, but people tend to leave them alone.....4

ATTACK:.........................7

SPEED:................................3

SIZE:................................3

DISOBEDIENCE:................8

I am afraid the Stinkdragon lays its eggs in a steaming pile of dragon poo

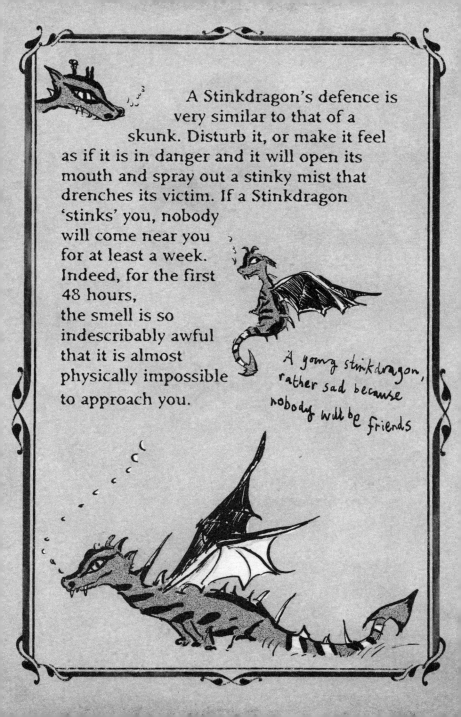

A Stinkdragon's defence is very similar to that of a skunk. Disturb it, or make it feel as if it is in danger and it will open its mouth and spray out a stinky mist that drenches its victim. If a Stinkdragon 'stinks' you, nobody will come near you for at least a week. Indeed, for the first 48 hours, the smell is so indescribably awful that it is almost physically impossible to approach you.

A young stinkdragon, rather sad because nobody will be friends

Mood - Dragons

~ STATISTICS ~

COLOURS: Constantly changing
ARMED WITH: Camouflage and the usual
talons and fire.
FEAR FACTOR:...........................4
ATTACK:.....................................6
SPEED:......................................10
SIZE:......................................3
DISOBEDIENCE:.......................7

Mood-dragon Nest,
with 4 eggs in it, 1 happy
1 sad, 1 embarrassed,
and 1 ABSOLUTELY FURIOUS

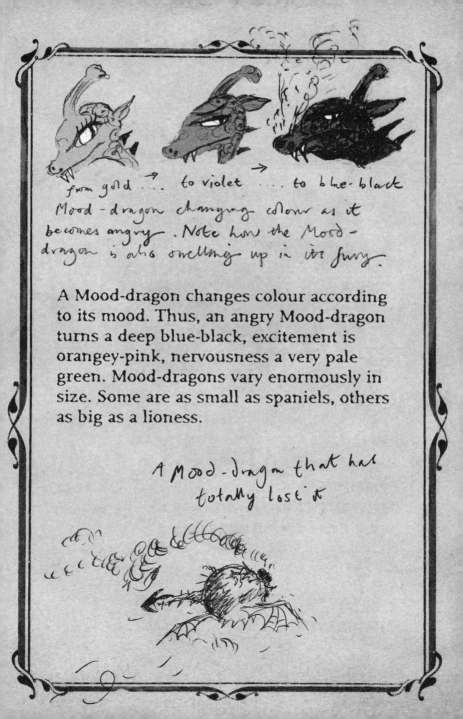

from gold →..... to violet ..... to blue-black
Mood-dragon changing colour as it
becomes angry. Note how the Mood-
dragon is also swelling up in its fury.

A Mood-dragon changes colour according
to its mood. Thus, an angry Mood-dragon
turns a deep blue-black, excitement is
orangey-pink, nervousness a very pale
green. Mood-dragons vary enormously in
size. Some are as small as spaniels, others
as big as a lioness.

A Mood-dragon that has
totally lost it

Driller-Dragons

~ STATISTICS ~

COLOURS: Black

ARMED WITH: Terrifying swivelling drill, and the usual teeth and talons.

FEAR FACTOR:........................8

ATTACK:...............................9

SPEED:.....................................6

SIZE:...6

DISOBEDIENCE:............................6

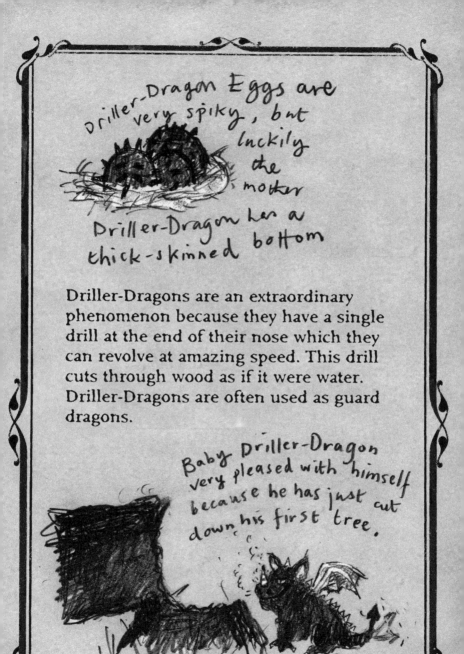

Driller-Dragon Eggs are very spiky, but luckily the mother Driller-Dragon has a thick-skinned bottom

Driller-Dragons are an extraordinary phenomenon because they have a single drill at the end of their nose which they can revolve at amazing speed. This drill cuts through wood as if it were water. Driller-Dragons are often used as guard dragons.

Baby Driller-Dragon very pleased with himself because he has just cut down his first tree.

Red-Hot Itchyworms

~ STATISTICS ~

COLOURS: Bright chilli red
ARMED WITH: A bite and a sting far more painful than a hornet.
FEAR FACTOR:......................4
ATTACK:................................4
SPEED:....................................5
SIZE:.......................................8
DISOBEDIENCE:...................3

Red-Hot Itchyworms are, as their name suggests, almost unbearably hot to the touch. They are blood-suckers, and when they get into a person's clothing they swarm all over the body in a pack, biting incessantly. An attack by Red-Hot Itchyworms is infinitely worse than having ants in your pants.

CUCKOO DRAGONS

~ STATISTICS ~

COLOURS: Aquamarine or turquoise
ARMED WITH: No particular extra weapons, but cuckoo dragons are very wily and intelligent.
FEAR FACTOR:............................. 3
ATTACK:.................................2
SPEED:....................................4
SIZE:......................................6
DISOBEDIENCE:......................5

The cuckoo dragon lays an egg in the nest of a bird, who then brings up the infant dragon as if it were her own baby, despite the growing size and strength of the imposter...

Sniffer Dragons

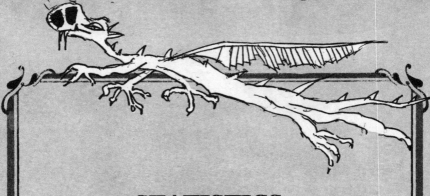

~ STATISTICS ~

COLOURS: Pale aquamarine

ARMED WITH: Large nose.

FEAR FACTOR: Sniffer dragons are not really fighters. They are used by the Murderous Tribe to track down enemies rather like blood-hounds...3

ATTACK:.........................6

SPEED............................4

SIZE:................................4

DISOBEDIENCE:................1

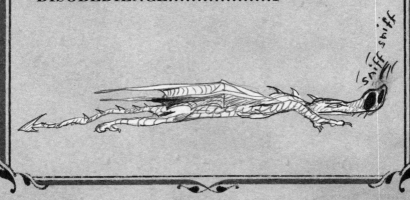

sniff sniff

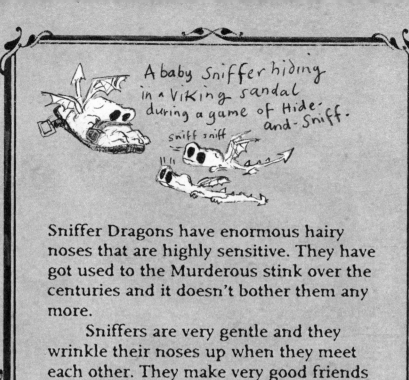

A baby Sniffer hiding in a Viking sandal during a game of Hide-and-Sniff.

sniff sniff

Sniffer Dragons have enormous hairy noses that are highly sensitive. They have got used to the Murderous stink over the centuries and it doesn't bother them any more.

Sniffers are very gentle and they wrinkle their noses up when they meet each other. They make very good friends and family pets.

sniff sniff

A nest of little Sniffers in an old tree root

Electricsquirms

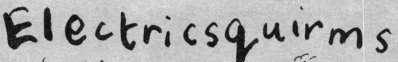

~ STATISTICS ~

COLOURS: Transparent
ARMED WITH: ELECTRICITY
FEAR FACTOR:............................4
ATTACK:...................................6
SPEED:....................................5
SIZE:..1
DISOBEDIENCE.....................3

This nanodragon is not aggressive, but it gives a truly terrible (although not fatal) electric shock when touched. Like their close cousins the Glow-worms, these creatures can be used as a source of light if no flame or candle is available.

Glow-worms

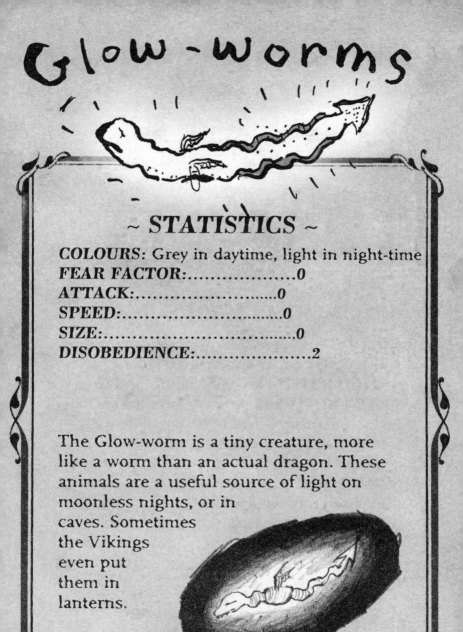

~ STATISTICS ~

COLOURS: Grey in daytime, light in night-time
FEAR FACTOR:....................*0*
ATTACK:........................*0*
SPEED:...........................*0*
SIZE:...............................*0*
DISOBEDIENCE:....................*2*

The Glow-worm is a tiny creature, more
like a worm than an actual dragon. These
animals are a useful source of light on
moonless nights, or in
caves. Sometimes
the Vikings
even put
them in
lanterns.

Shortwing Squirrelserpent

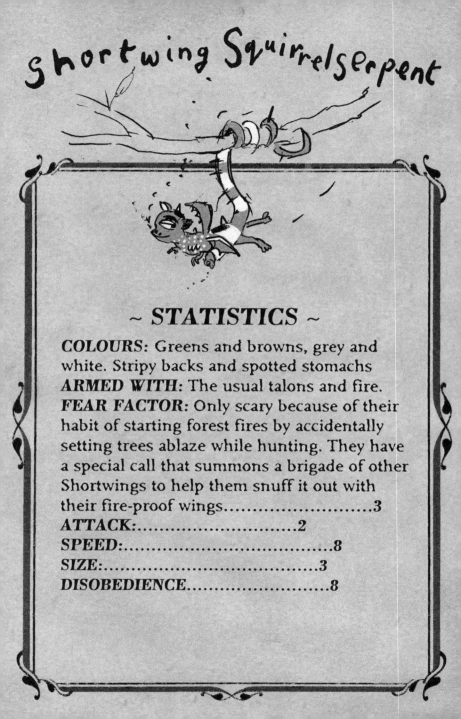

~ STATISTICS ~

COLOURS: Greens and browns, grey and white. Stripy backs and spotted stomachs

ARMED WITH: The usual talons and fire.

FEAR FACTOR: Only scary because of their habit of starting forest fires by accidentally setting trees ablaze while hunting. They have a special call that summons a brigade of other Shortwings to help them snuff it out with their fire-proof wings..........................3

ATTACK:...........................*2*

SPEED:...................................8

SIZE:......................................*3*

DISOBEDIENCE..........................8

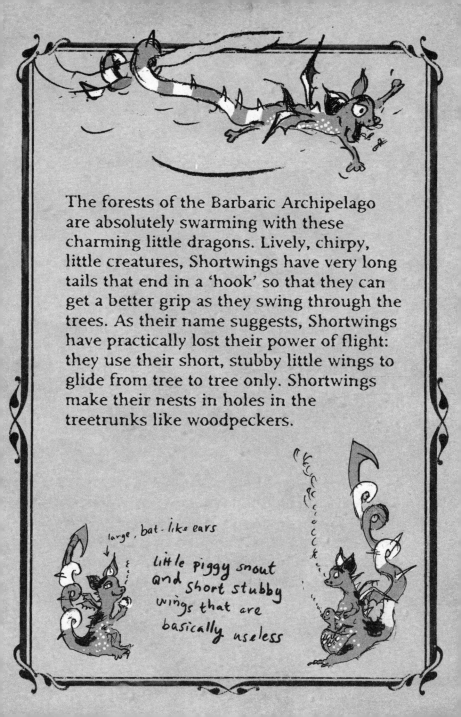

The forests of the Barbaric Archipelago are absolutely swarming with these charming little dragons. Lively, chirpy, little creatures, Shortwings have very long tails that end in a 'hook' so that they can get a better grip as they swing through the trees. As their name suggests, Shortwings have practically lost their power of flight: they use their short, stubby little wings to glide from tree to tree only. Shortwings make their nests in holes in the treetrunks like woodpeckers.

large, bat-like ears

little piggy snout and short stubby wings that are basically useless

Vampire Dragons

~ STATISTICS ~

COLOURS: Black, dark grey, midnight blue
ARMED WITH: Two front teeth and mouth with a powerful suction.
FEAR FACTOR:............................7
ATTACK:....................................7
SPEED:......................................4
SIZE:...2
DISOBEDIENCE:.........................9

These nocturnal bloodsucking creatures will attack any large mammal reindeer, sheep or even humans. One Vampire alone cannot kill, but an attack by an entire vex is very often fatal. The victim does not wake up during an attack because the Vampire anaesthetises the skin before it bites.

Stealth Dragons

~ STATISTICS ~

COLOURS: Constantly changing
ARMED WITH: Projectile fire rockets, explosive burn streams and finger-lightning.
FEAR FACTOR:...........................8
ATTACK:.................................9
SPEED:..................................9
SIZE:.....................................8
DISOBEDIENCE:.......................5

Unfortunately we cannot show a picture of the Stealth Dragon because it is so well camouflaged that it is practically invisible. These dragons are very useful if you wish to sneak up on an enemy without being detected.

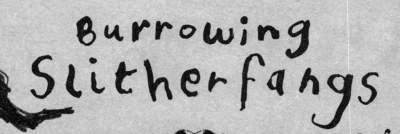

Burrowing Slitherfangs

~ STATISTICS ~

COLOURS: Brown, grey and pink, and like its close cousin the Strangulator, covered in yicky slime and goo.

ARMED WITH: The Slitherfang pulls its victim under the ground, where the victim suffocates, and is then devoured.

FEAR FACTOR: Once a Slitherfang has grabbed you by the ankle, you are pretty much a goner...**10**

DEFENCES: Smaller Slitherfangs are sometimes attacked by enormous Creatures like Seadragons Giganticus Maximius, who grab them by the tentacles and pull them out of the ground like worms. But mostly Slitherfangs dig too deep too quickly to be caught.. **9**

SPEED: Frighteningly quick......... **10**

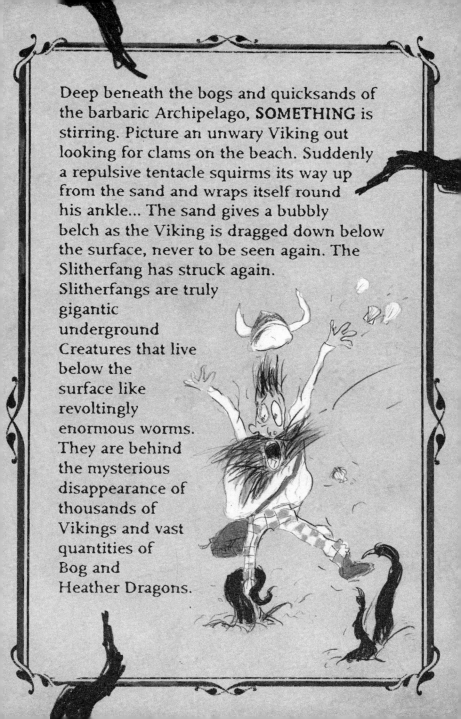

Deep beneath the bogs and quicksands of the barbaric Archipelago, **SOMETHING** is stirring. Picture an unwary Viking out looking for clams on the beach. Suddenly a repulsive tentacle squirms its way up from the sand and wraps itself round his ankle... The sand gives a bubbly belch as the Viking is dragged down below the surface, never to be seen again. The Slitherfang has struck again.

Slitherfangs are truly gigantic underground Creatures that live below the surface like revoltingly enormous worms. They are behind the mysterious disappearance of thousands of Vikings and vast quantities of Bog and Heather Dragons.

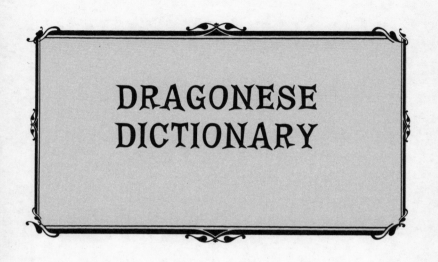

DRAGONESE
DICTIONARY

DRAGONESE DICTIONARY

a	un
a little	piddly
a lot	muggly
again	wummortime
agony	ow-lika-dentipull
all right	okey dokey
am	is
and	plus
anyway	wateva
are	est
armour	joosqueeze-protector
autumn	fallings
axe	chopper

bad mood	thunderpuffs issa zapping
beach	drybits
because	parsk
bed	sleepy-slab
bedroom	zuzzspot

DRAGONESE DICTIONARY

bee	buzzer
beer/mead	{ giggle juice silly juice wobble juice }
belch/burp	gobfart
bet	gambla
better	perky
big	giganticus
bird	song-munch
biscuit	snik-snak
bite someone on the bottom	yum-yum on di bum
bite someone on the finger	yum-yum on di thumb
bite someone on the stomach	yum-yum on di tum
bits	tiddles
blanket	snugger
blood	{ oozejoos scarlett joos }
bog	runner-sink
bogeys	sniffersludge
bone	white branch
bottom	{ botti bum dubbli much }
bow and arrow	pluckit plus forkend
brave	lacksmart (lit. foolish)
breakfast	earlymunch

DRAGONESE DICTIONARY

burgle	snickle
burrow	gaff
burrow, to	buggle
burst into tears	do di girly boo-hoo

can	may
can I?	goffa
carry	cunga
carrots (and all kinds of veg.)	snorey-munch
cat	miaowla / miaow-miaow
catch	catcha
ceiling	airtop
chair	bum-support
chase	chassa
cheese	moo-poos block
chimney	scorchspot
chocolate	chocklush
choose	choosa
clever	quicksmart
cloak	swirlaround
close	snap

DRAGONESE DICTIONARY

cloud	wet clump
cold	shivers
cosy	toastiboili
cow	horn-creamer milky-dangler moo-munch
crabs	crawl pinches
crackling	zapping
crawl	claggle
cucumber	greenburger

dad	pappa
dagger	pricker
dance	tootsieing
day	dunning
death	big dreamtime
deer	prickle-burger
definitely	doubly doubly
delicious	scrumplush
dipped	dunkings

DRAGONESE DICTIONARY

disgusting/ revolting	yuck-yuck
disgusting, really	doubly yuck-yuck
do not care	isna burped
dog	dim-woof
don't	na
don't like	na likeit
door	slammer
down	moleway
dragon	{ greenclaw greenblood
drink	glugga

ears	squearers
earth	squelchy bit
eat	{ eaty gobbla munch-munch scrumming
enemies	piss-people
eyes	peepers

DRAGONESE DICTIONARY

far	staraway
farts	{ botty-crackers buttok-thunder smelly-breezers
fat	{ wobbliflesh jellibelli
favourite	bestest
feather	flyfluff
feet	runners
fern	stridescrapers
fetch	grabba
fire	{ warmadi-tootsies scorch-crackle
fire, to set	flicka-flame
fish	saltswimmys
fit/put	parka
floor	dust holder
flower	buzz-munch
fly	flip-flap
follow	two step
food	grubbings
footsteps	slow-mo-pop
for	par

DRAGONESE DICTIONARY

forget	rubout
fork	poker
friend	freundlee

ghost	fella o di dreamtime
give	giva
glass	lookthru
goodbye	toodleoon
grass	green stuff
greedy	overmunch
gross	poo-poo
guy	piss-person

haddock	stinkfish
hair	gogglechoke
hands	reechers
happy	smirkling
harbour	landscoop
have	ava

DRAGONESE DICTIONARY

he	hissa
head	{ brainbox noddle puzzler
headache	ow-indi-brainbox
hear	{ earwig squear
heart	joossqueeze
heather	purple stuff
hello	howdeedoodeethere
helmet	puzzle-protector
here	vola
honey	buzzjoos
horse	neigh-munch
hot dogs/ sausages	warm woofs *(made from venison)*
house	{ hoosus wingless gaff
how?	horra?
how do you do?	farin okey?
hug	vomit-belly squeezes
human beings	{ da wingless land prisoners no-brainers skyless dirt grubbers
hungry	belly-scream
hunting	prickin

DRAGONESE DICTIONARY

I	me
I do like it	me like it
in	ipps
in this	indi
insects	scuttles
inside	inna
islands	drybits
is not	snotta
it's not	sna

jacket	grubwarmer
joking	tickling

kind	keendlee
kiss	swappa da yucki lip-juice

DRAGONESE DICTIONARY

kitchen	munchspot
knees	clackers
knife	slicer
know	coglet

laugh	do di chuckli ha-has
last time	pastime
lead	first step
legs	striders
legs hurting	ow-indi-tootsies
less than	plus piddly
lesson	snorer
lie	greenblood-speek
like	com
liked	likeit
little	{ ickle { min
live	folda (lit. means fold)
lobsters	front pinches
look	goggle
lose	leafbeyind
loud	fortissimo
love	'e's alright reely
lucky	doublesix

DRAGONESE DICTIONARY

marsh	oozer
master	yellfatter
mean	snakesnipper
meet	greety
middle	middling
milk	moo-joos
moon	dark-peeper *(lit. eye of the dark)*
more than	luggly
mother	mama
mouse	squeaky-snack
mouth	gob
my	{ me / mi
myself	meselva

name	calda
nanodragons	pesti-stings
nest	gaff
next door	ensweet

DRAGONESE DICTIONARY

night	zuzztime
no	nee-ah
no problem	easipeasilemonsqueezi
nobody	neverman
nose	sniffer
not	isna
not at all	fiddleplum

ocean	wetworld
OK	okey
old/wrinkly	crumply
once	wun time
or	oo
out	opps
oysters	saltsicks

paper	frickle
pen	frickle-scratch

DRAGONESE DICTIONARY

pig	squeal-munch
plate	plonker
please	pishyou
pleased	heeby-jeebies
poisonous	{ ow-in-di-tummy wobblediguts
poo	cack-cack
pooing	crappa
porridge	uglysludge
pyjamas	jim-jams

rabbit	randifloss
rain	{ blue leak thunderman drip-drops *(lit. Thor's tears)*
remember	regurgle
right	oopla
right now	snip-snap
romans	hairless no-brainers
room	hovel
rug	wipe
rumbling	lardi-gurgles
run	quick-mo

DRAGONESE DICTIONARY

saucepan	munchboil
scratch	scarlet strokings
scream	yowlyshreekers
scrummy	yum-yumindutum
sea	wettings
see	{ goggla peepa
sheep	dim-fluff
shells	squergleboxes
ship/sail	puffcatcher
shoe	runnerbox
shout	roarspeek
shy	shushrose
sick	{ weeklyweed wobble-di-guts
sit	parka di botty
sky	bluetop
sleep	zip di peepers
sleeping	zuzzing
smell	sniffa
smile	curlup di gob
sneaky	tipclaw

DRAGONESE DICTIONARY

sneeze	spray di brain-goo
snot	brain-goo
snow	dandruff-di-woden
so	too
spear	plunger
spit	gobba
splat	splosh
spoon	scooper
spring	wettings
start	gogo
starvation	gobbledesert
steal	swappit
stinks	yucksniff
stomach	grubwasher
stone	{ grittybit landmake
stormclouds	thunderpuffs
stream	wet crackle
stupid	lacksmart
summer	boilings
sun	hot o di world
sunshine	dazzleit
swim	wet-flap
sword	flashpricker

DRAGONESE DICTIONARY

table	{ munchy-holder { munch-support
tail	forkwaver
take	tacka
talons/toenails	scrapers
tantrum, to have a	do di wobbly screamers
temper, to lose your	{ do di heeby jeebys { do di hissifittings { do di screemiberserkers
thank you	thankee
that	da
that bad	tootoo
that way	vuzza
the	di
there	dere
thirsty	dry-gurgs
this way	vizza
Thor	Thunderman
three years old	par twa freezings
threw up/sick	chuck-it-up
throat	goggle
throw	bunga

DRAGONESE DICTIONARY

time	tick tock
tiptoe	shushstep
tired	zuzzready
toilet	crapspot
tongue	forkspeeker
too	tow
tree	bluescraper/leafings
tummy	grubwasher
tummyache	ow-indi-grubwasher

up	godway

vegetables	snory munch
vengeful	grimful
very	{ bigtime buckets
viking	hairy no-brainers

DRAGONESE DICTIONARY

wake up	peepers undo
walk	slow-mo
want	{ needy
	{ wanti
was	woz
water	gurglelap
wave	wetting wrinkle
what?	warra?
when?	tarra?
where?	yarra?
which?	wotcha?
whisper	shushspeek
who?	hoody?
whose?	hossa?
why?	quera?
wind	thorpuff
window	air square
wings	{ flip-flaps
	{ gliders
winkles	snotting-gum
winter	freezings
with	wi
worms	squergles

DRAGONESE DICTIONARY

yes	yessee
you	{ ta yow

OLOURS

black	squidink
blue	seasky
green	leafy
purple	broos
red	{ crimson rose scarlet
white	white
yellow	butter colour

DRAGONESE DICTIONARY

Know your NUMBERS

Counting in Dragonese all the way up to googles

one	oos
two	doos
three	twa
four	far
five	fiff
six	sick
seven	soccer
eight	accer
nine	ninner
ten	dim
eleven	liver
twelve	twiver
thirteen	twaver
fourteen	fartix
fifteen	fiftix
sixteen	sixtix
seventeen	soccertix
eighteen	accertix
nineteen	ninnertix
twenty	twimmy
twenty-one	twimmy-oos
twenty-two	twimmy-doos

DRAGONESE DICTIONARY

twenty-three	twimmy-twa
twenty-four	twimmy-far
twenty-five	twimmy-fiff
twenty-six	twimmy-sick
twenty-seven	twimmy-soccer
twenty-eight	twimmy-accer
twenty-nine	twimmy-ninner
thirty	thrimmy
forty	farty
fifty	fiffy
sixty	sicky
seventy	socky
eighty	acky
ninety	ninny
a hundred	un ponder
a hundred and one	un ponder plus oos
a thousand	un wonder
a hundred thousand	un ponder o wonders
a million	un marvel
a hundred million	un ponder o marvels
a zillion	un boggle
a google	un stagger-boggle

the largest number anyone has
ever thought of, and then add one:
un tricksy blow-di-brainbox boggle plus oos

Conversations with Toothless

Getting to Know you...

Howdeedoodethere
Hello

Me calda Toothless, farin okey?
My name is Toothless, how do you do?

Me calda T-T-toothless

Watcha calda?
What is your name?

Woh crumply est ta?
How old are you? (lit. how wrinkly are you?)

Me is crumply par twa freezings
I am three years old

Wa folda da flip-flaps?
Where do you live? (lit. where do you fold your wings?)

Me folda indi leafings
I live in this tree

Me folda indi randifloss gaff
I live in this rabbit burrow
(Me gobbla di randifloss)
(I ate the rabbit)

Me folda wi me freundlee, Hiccup
I live with my friend Hiccup

Hissa okey, par un no-brainer
He's OK, for a human being

Hissa na yucksniff tootoo
He doesn't smell that bad

Na com da piss-person Snotlout
Not like that dreadful guy Snotlout

Hissa yucksniff plusplus da un fif-sunning-
crumply stinkfish, dunkings
inna cack-cack di Gronckle
*He stinks worse than a
five-day-old haddock dipped
in Gronckle poo*

Me isna tickling
I'm not joking

hissa
YUCKSNIFF

Da pastime me greety
hiss, da yucksniff
woz too greasypiss,
me is disclose da chuck-it-up
*The last time we met, the smell
was so bad I nearly threw up*

me is disclose
da chuck-it-up

Plus, yow goggla da sniffer on da piss-person?
And did you see the nose on that guy?

Da sniffer issa too giganticus,
yow may parka un greenburger up dere
That nose is so big, you could fit a
cucumber up there

Me coglet, parsk me parka un dere
meselva
I know because I
put one there
myself

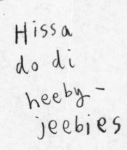

Me coglet,
parsk me
parka un
dere meselva

Hissa zuzzing
He was sleeping

May hissa
peepers undo
snipsnap
But he woke up

Hissa do di heeby-jeebies
He wasn't very pleased

Hissa
do di
heeby-
jeebies

Me na coglet comma, may hissa na likeit me never
I don't know why, but he's never really liked me.

Me na coglet comma, may hissa na likeit me never,

T-T-T-T-T-T-Tee hee hee hee hee
Ha ha ha

Me isna burped
I couldn't care less

t-t-t
t-tee-hee

When you are ILL...

Oooooh, harditips di Thunderman
OOOOOh, thumbnails of Thor

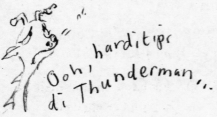

Ooh, harditips
di Thunderman,,

Toothless ava
ow-indi-brainbox
I have a headache

Or,
Toothless ava
ow-indi-tootsies
My legs are hurting

Toothless ava
ow-in-di-
tootsies

Toothless ava
ow indi-brainbox

Or, most likely,
Toothless ava
ow-indi-grubwasher
I have a tummyache

Toothless ava
ow-in-di-grubwasher
OW OW OW

Me isna tickling
I'm not messing with you

Issa ow-lika-dentipull
It's agony

Sna parsk me na likeit da
uppit da sleepy-slab
*It's not because I don't
want to get out of bed*

Sna parsk issa toastiboili inna sleepy-slab
It's not because it's all cosy in bed

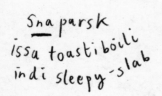

Sna parsk me na likeit outy indi Wetworld prickin di
saltswimmys indi Prickin Snorer par wobbliflesh
Gobber di Gobfart
*It's not because I don't want to go out there hunting fish
in a Hunting Lesson for big fat Gobber the Belch*

Indi Thunderman drip-drops
In the rain (lit. Thor's tears)

Plus di shivers
And the cold

Issa parsk me issa big dreamtime
It's because I am dying

Toothless dreamtime plus neverman issa burped
I'm dying and nobody cares

Me grubwasher issa weeklyweed buckets
My stomach is very very sick

(PAUSE)

Me sniffa da earlymunch?
Can I smell breakfast?

OOOoooooooh, warm-woofs plus
saltsicks issa Toothless's BESTEST
*Oooooooh, sausages and oysters is
my FAVOURITE*

*Issa parsk
me issa big
dreamtime*

Me has buckets di belly-scream me may gobbla di
horn-creamers
I am so hungry, I could eat a cow

Belly-scream... PLUS dreamtime
Hungry... AND dying

Toothless ava earlymunch indi sleepy-slab?
Can I have breakfast in bed?

Yi sna?
Why not?

Yow issa snakenipper Yellfatter
You are a very mean Master

Wi un squeezeblood di landmake
With a heart of stone

Plus yow may drip-drop buckets time yow sadly min
greenblood issa dreamtime frim gobbledesert plus
ow-indi-grubwasher
*And you will regret this when your poor little dragon has
died of starvation and tummyache*

May doublesix par yow, me issa min perky
But luckily for you, I'm feeling a little better

(flies out of bed, miraculously recovered)

May me ava buzzjoos wi me saltsicks?
Can I have honey on my oysters?

Hiccup's arch enemy is

Alvin the Treacherous

Ex-Chief of the Outcast Tribe

Alvin's greed and malevolence have led to him becoming smaller and smaller over the years.

His arm was cut off by Grimbeard the Ghastly. The stomach juices of the Monstrous Strangulator have caused all his hair to fall out.

And he has lost both a hand and an eye during an unfortunate encounter with some Sharkworms…

At this rate, there'll be nothing left of him at all.

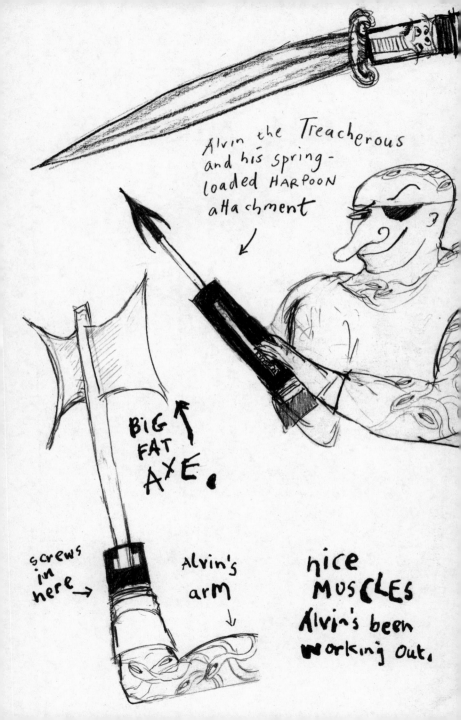

Alvin the Treacherous
and his spring-
loaded HARPOON
attachment

BIG
FAT
AXE.

screws
in
here →

Alvin's
arm
↓

nice
MUSCLES
Alvin's been
working out.

Alvin was recently swallowed up by a Fire-Dragon, who then dived into a volcano...

Surely even **Alvin** could not return from this experience to fight another day?

Watch out for the next volume of Hiccup's memoirs, **How to Ride a Dragon's Storm**

This is Cressida, age 9, writing on the island.

Cressida Cowell grew up in London and on a small, uninhabited island off the west coast of Scotland where she spent her time writing stories, fishing for things to eat, and exploring the island looking for dragons. She was convinced that there were dragons living on the island, and has been fascinated by them ever since.

www.cressidacowell.com

HOWDEEDOODEETHERE!

For your latest news on all things dragon and Cressida Cowell please follow:

 @cressidacowellauthor

 @cressidacowell

 facebook.com/
cressidacowellauthor

Toodleoon for now...

'Cowell's How to Train Your Dragon books are national treasures.'
Amanda Craig, *The Times*

'Bound to become a modern classic.'
Independent

'Always thrilling, funny and brilliantly illustrated.' ***Daily Express***

'Cressida Cowell is a splendid story-teller ... young readers are lucky to have her.'
Books for Keeps

'One of the greatest inventions of modern children's literature.'
Julia Eccleshare, LoverReading4kids

'Funny, outrageous and will lure in the most reluctant reader.' ***Spectator***

'As with the best children's literature, these books are about much bigger things: endurance, loyalty, friendship and love.' ***Daily Telegraph***

'Cowell's loopy scattershot imagination is as compelling as ever.' ***Financial Times***

CRESSIDA COWELL
HOW TO TRAIN YOUR
DRAGON

READ HICCUP'S GUIDE TO DRAGON SPECIES ...

Full of dragon profiles and tips on how to ride and train them ... a **MUST READ** for anyone who wants to know more about dragons.

LOOK OUT FOR
CRESSIDA COWELL'S
NEW SERIES

The WIZARDS of ONCE

Once there Was Magic...

This is the story of a young boy Wizard, and a young girl Warrior, who have been taught to hate each other like poison.

#wizardsofonce